Seneschal Publishing; Oakley, California
www.seneschalpublishing.com
Twitter: @SeneschalBooks

Cover Photo Courtesy of Sean Christopher Flansbaum
www.flansdigital.com

ISBN paperback: 978-0-9981350-2-1
ISBN eBook: 978-0-9981350-3-8

First Paperback Edition

Printed in the United States of America

Other Books by Michael Chrobak

'Brother Thomas and the Guardians of Zion' Series

Book One: Foundations of Faith
Book Two: The Paladin of Panama
Book Three: The Guardians Crest
Book Four: Apocalypse (Coming Spring 2019)

'Where Angels' Series

Where Angels Dwell
Where Angels Cry (Coming Winter 2019)

For my loving wife, Janice
Without you I would not exist

Chapter One
Rebirth

Jesus answered, "Truly, truly, I say to you, unless one is born again he cannot see the Kingdom of God" - John 3:3

Friday, September 30

"Good morning, Daddy!"

"I know that voice," Mark thought as his mind struggled back to consciousness.

He was in a fog. A deep, dense, colorless fog. Through the mist, a fragment of memory appeared. That voice he heard, it belonged to his daughter. But she was four hundred miles away at college, wasn't she? He wasn't supposed to see her until Thanksgiving. As far as he knew, it was still September.

"What is she doing here?" Mark wondered, suddenly aware he didn't know where *here* was.

Slowly, Mark regained clarity. It felt like waking from a dream. Yet no dream before had held him captive like this. He could hear movement nearby, and felt the presence of someone at his side. He tried opening his eyes. Nothing happened. Even if he focused as hard as he could, he saw nothing but vague splashes of light. Everything was a blur.

And then, a moment of recognition. It felt like there was something stuck down his throat. Mark tried pulling on it. It wouldn't move. Suddenly, he realized, neither had he. He only thought he had pulled it. His

1

arms had never moved. The fog closed in again, consciousness faded once more. He returned to the darkness.

When the fog lifted once more, he wasn't sure how much time had gone by. The first thing he noticed was the sound of more voices. He also thought he could feel someone holding his hand. Mark still couldn't see, though. Once more he sensed movement around him. The fog parted further, consciousness flooded in. He felt his eyes blink.

So, they were open! But, why couldn't he see?

"Good morning, Mark! How about we take out that tube today?" a voice said from somewhere near him.

Mark didn't know this voice. It was gentle and soft, with an accent he couldn't quite place.

"What tube?"

"Who is that speaking?"

"Where am I?"

He nodded. At least, he thought he did. It was hard to tell if his body was responding. He still felt numb. The harder he fought for clarity, the more his mind scrambled, like puzzle pieces in a box. Questions poured in, but no answers followed.

"Who are these people?"

"Why can't I see?"

"What happened to me?"

Mark searched his memories in vain, finding nothing but more fog. He considered that he really wasn't awake. When he felt his hand being moved again, he could tell that much was real. Someone was holding it. Someone warm, soft, and familiar.

"Hey, hon," a voice said from close by, "So, it's Friday. You've missed a few days."

"*That's my wife's voice,*" Mark realized. "*What did she mean, I missed a few days? What's going on?*"

Clarity came, and left, and came again. He couldn't hold it for long. Mark was on the edge of panic. He had to find the answers to all these questions.

"*What's the last thing I recall?*" he wondered silently, searching for even the smallest fragment. "*Oh yeah. Pain. Tremendous pain. And fear.*"

He remembered.

Tuesday, September 27

Mark had been feeling under the weather for about a week. It hadn't felt serious, though. And he should know. As a child he had struggled constantly with one virus or another. A sinus infection one year, strep throat the next. Bronchitis, mono, you name it, Mark had had it. Even pneumonia once, back in fourth or fifth grade. What he had been feeling wasn't like any of those. It had been just a minor cough and a low grade fever. He had felt weak, like he had no energy. He hadn't had chills or body aches like if it had been the flu. He hadn't been coughing up anything like when he had bronchitis. He had considered that it was probably just a cold. Most likely something he had picked it up from his wife. Jennifer was an elementary school teacher and was always bringing something home. Whatever it was, Mark had been sure that it would pass.

But it hadn't passed. It had gotten worse. Earlier that morning he had coughed up blood. Not much, just enough to consider he should have made an appointment with his doctor. Unfortunately, it had been too late for that. By the time he and Jennifer had finished dinner, he had already been in distress. The next coughing spasm had brought a sudden, sharp pain to the left side of his chest. It had felt like he had broken a rib. The

3

pain had gone away after a few minutes, only to return an hour later. That time, it hadn't stopped.

Every breath had hurt. The more he had struggled, the worse it had become. Mark had never experienced pain that severe. He had endured various cuts, scrapes, broken bones and torn muscles, all without losing a single day of work. But the pain that night was beyond anything before. He had been barely able to keep from collapsing. Jennifer had tried to get him into the car, but Mark had no longer been able to stand. Instead, she had dialed 911. The firefighters had arrived within minutes, bursting into the house and throwing questions at him.

"Can you point to where it hurts?"

"When did it start?"

"How bad is it?"

"Did you fall recently?"

"Did you hear anything snap or pop?"

Mark had answered as best he could, but it had been difficult. Speaking had meant breathing, and breathing hurt. The firefighters had tried guessing what it might have been. Gallstones. Pulled muscle. They had ruled out something heart related. The pain had been in the wrong spot for that. He hadn't cared if they had guessed right or not. He had only wanted one thing: make it stop. He had asked them to do exactly that several times. Each time they had replied, "We will. Soon."

The paramedics then arrived with another round of questions. They had performed a quick assessment of his vitals before loading him on a gurney and taking him outside.

"So, which hospital do you want?" one of the paramedics had asked once Mark was loaded in the ambulance.

"The closest one," Mark had replied, having considered that time was of some urgency.

It had taken a few minutes to get him set up. They had shaved his arm, inserted an IV, and started pain meds. By the time they had arrived at the hospital, the meds had kicked in. He remembered being more than a bit loopy.

"This isn't the pizza place!" Mark had blurted out as they removed him from the ambulance. His mind had started to blur. Only one thing remained clear.

Pain.

It had hurt when they striped off his clothes. It had hurt even more when they had taken the x-ray. But the CT scan, that had been the worst. He hadn't been able to stop screaming. Next, he had been wheeled into an elevator and moved into a room. There he had met the nurse assigned to him. The nurse had placed a mask over his nose and mouth to help him breathe, and then inserted a catheter. Mark had drifted in and out of consciousness. When the pain got worse, he had requested more meds.

The pain had been so severe he had begun to black out. Breathing had become impossible. A flood of nurses had poured into his room, pulling his bed into the hall, and rushing him back to the elevator.

Although he hadn't been aware at the time, Mark had been transported to Intensive Care. The doctor in charge asked permission to insert a breathing tube. Mark remembered shouting in reply.

"Save me!"

Friday, September 30

Mark's attention returned to the present. His eyes blinked as he tried to clear the tears.

"So, those were the two days I missed," he thought, giving his wife's hand a gentle squeeze.

Everything from that final memory late Tuesday night until just a few moments ago was gone. It was as if he didn't exist. Mark now understood. He had been sedated. Apparently, he had been a hard patient to sedate. His wife was in the process of telling him how, even in his weakened condition, he had fought against the drugs for two hours. They had to strap him to the hospital bed to keep him from hurting himself. Still, he fought. She told him how the doctors informed her it would take thirty minutes, and how they had asked her to wait outside. Mark felt bad for Jennifer. How nervous she must have been pacing that hallway, waiting for any word on his status after those first thirty minutes had passed.

Mark continued to float back and forth in the fog. Some moments were clear, others were lost in the stupor of medication. At some point the nurses had removed the breathing tube. He wasn't sure exactly when. They also must have helped him out of bed, because he was now sitting in a chair.

In between the random moments of consciousness, one thing became clear: the pain was gone. Mark thought that perhaps it was still there, hidden behind the veil of drugs still dampening his mind. His wife had told him he was on a constant drip of morphine, along with several other drugs. She ran through the list, explaining what each one was for, but her words barely registered.

"So, where exactly am I?" he asked when she paused a moment.

"You're in the ICU at Sutter," Jennifer replied.

"I kind of figured that, but, what happened?"

"You almost died," she said, a glossy sheen in her

eyes. "They gave you less than twenty-percent chance you would pull through."

Mark wondered what Jennifer had felt when she had heard that news. He could only imagine her fear.

"How?" he asked, squeezing her left hand as her right hand wiped tears from her eyes.

"You had pneumonia. Your left lung was more than half filled with fluid. That's why you couldn't breathe," she told him. "They had to install that tube just to keep you alive. Oh, hon, I didn't know what to do. We've never discussed if you would want machines to keep you alive or not. I was just so scared."

The pain and fear she was holding was evident. Jennifer had made some difficult choices the last few days. He had no idea how he would ever make it up to her.

"That's not all," she continued. "Since your lungs weren't processing enough oxygen, your other organs started to fail. Plus, your blood was turning acidic. Basically your body was responding as if you had already died."

Mark wanted nothing more than to wrap his arms around his wife, hold her until the fear and sadness she had had to swallow poured out through her tears. His body still felt heavy, leaden, and unresponsive. All he could manage was another weak squeeze of her hand. For now, that would have to be enough.

There had to be something he could do, some way of helping her through her despair, to make her believe he was stronger than he felt. As one of his nurses came in the room, he found his chance.

Humor! If he started joking, she would know he was okay. That's what he did when he was in a good

7

mood. He hoped it would work.

"Well, you're looking much better today! How do you feel?" the nurse asked.

"Pretty good. I'm ready to go dancing!" he joked.

"Oh, really?" the nurse laughed, helping him back into bed. "Well, let's take a look at you."

She wrapped a blood pressure cuff around his arm and stuck a thermometer in his mouth. Mark glanced at the display on the machine at his side. His blood pressure was elevated, far higher than he had ever seen before. The nurse pulled back his blanket to check his torso and legs.

"Any sign of swelling?" she asked, squeezing his legs gently.

"Only my biceps. I look like Schwarzenegger now," Mark said, trying to imitate the Austrian actor.

He glanced to where his wife and daughter stood watching. They were smiling. Although he still didn't feel well at all, he wasn't going to let them worry. Not one more moment. If he could help it, they wouldn't know how bad he felt.

The nurse left, satisfied that Mark had shown some improvement since his last set of readings. Mark yawned, and then stretched. Weariness was taking hold once more. Slowly, he drifted back to sleep. This became a pattern that repeated over and over again throughout the day. A nurse would come in, wake him up, check his vitals, adjust his meds, then leave, and he would fall asleep once more. While he was awake, he did his best to smile and joke, trying to retain consciousness as long as he could. Eventually, the physical strain and numbness from the medications would win, and he would drift away.

Each time he woke, the fog surrounding his mind had lifted a little more. The sedation was wearing off, and clarity was returning. At one point, late at night when the hospital was quiet, he was alone. At least, he was the only one awake. Jennifer was curled up in a chair in the corner, sleeping as best as she could. His daughter had left a few hours ago. She too needed rest. No one had slept much during the three days he had been sedated. Now, for the first time since coming out of his stupor, Mark couldn't sleep. He felt just as tired and weary as he had all day, but his mind was on fire.

A tiny thread of memory had flashed by, just long enough to draw him in. The thread wrapped itself around other thoughts and memories, searching for anything that fit. As small pieces began to weave back together, Mark had a realization. At some point while he was unconscious, while his body fought to thwart his death, his spirit had stood before the Throne of God.

This realization wasn't a joyous one. It wasn't a memory of walking around in heaven like he had seen in the movies. It didn't include angels or long lost relatives who needed to share secret messages only he would understand. It was deeper than that. God had spoken to him. The words he recalled, though simple, now shocked him to the core.

"Mark...you've done well living a good life. But you weren't created to live a good life. You were created for a great one."

That was it. Nothing about what this 'great' life was supposed to include. No directions on what to do, or who to speak to, or where to go. Just those few, brief sentences. He felt them repeat over and over through every cell in his body. Tiny flashes of energy pulsed like so many fireflies on a warm, summer night. This wasn't just a casual statement, like a gentle reminder to be kind, or to have faith. This was a challenge, an edict from the one who had given him life more than fifty years ago. He shuddered under the weight of this thought. Not from fear, but from anticipation, wonder, and awe.

For so long he had wondered about his purpose, why he had been created. He had never felt like he fit in anywhere, or with anyone. There was always something that didn't feel quite right, as if he had to protect himself. He knew there were times in life when he should have made a different choice, but he hadn't. He had always taken the safest path, the one that kept him from being noticed. Whenever he reached a point where he felt trusted or needed, he had always moved on. He had been more than willing to accept just a good life. A simple, easy life. He had never needed to be someone of importance.

But now he began to think otherwise. He began to feel that he had let himself down, let others down, and even let God down. He recalled moments from his youth when he had felt an almost constant urging to do something brave. And, there were a few scattered moments when he knew he had been brave. Vague memories of standing up for what he believed in. Challenges that had forced him to take risks. Relationships when he had let his heart be exposed.

He couldn't recall exactly when that all changed. If there was a specific moment when he had risked too much, opened up to far, or had been hurt somehow, it was trapped too far down for his muddled mind to retrieve. There was one thing he did know for sure, though. From this day forward, he was going to change.

He would learn to be brave once more, to take more chances, even if that meant accepting the risk of being hurt. He would let others see who he really was, once he discovered it again for himself. From this point forward, there would be no more safe choices. Every decision would be made with meaning and purpose. If one didn't, he would do something to ensure that it did. From here on 'good enough' wouldn't be a phrase he would accept.

There was only one place to start. He had to get right with himself. And to get right with himself, he knew he would first have to get right with God. Mark needed reconciliation now more than he ever had in his life. There were simply too many burdens weighing him down. With that thought in mind, he closed his eyes, and drifted to sleep.

Saturday, October 1

Morning came and Mark woke. Around him the hospital was waking, too. The day shift nurses were beginning to arrive. They began their rounds paired up with the night shift nurses who were on their way out. They walked the hallway outside the rooms, reviewing each patient being handed over. Mark could hear them outside his room.

"The next patient is Mark. He was admitted on the twenty-seventh with abdominal pain. Tests revealed severe pneumonia in the left lung. He went into respiratory failure and was intubated early on the twenty-eighth. The tube was removed yesterday morning..."

The conversation continued as the night nurse ran down the list of medications and therapies Mark had been prescribed. And then the pair moved on to the next room. Eventually the day shift nurse came in and introduced herself, then went about the process of getting him ready for the day. That meant another round of vitals, checking him over for any signs of swelling or bruising, and ensuring his meds were still flowing. The activity woke Jennifer. As she rubbed her eyes and stretched, Mark was anxious to share what he had discovered during the night. He waited until the nurse finished, and they were once again alone. When she left, he turned on his side to face his wife.

"So, you know how you said I almost died?" he asked her softly.

"Yeah. What about it?" she replied.

"I think I kinda did. Well, more like there was a period of time when I wasn't really in my body."

"What do you mean?"

Mark turned to look at his wife. Her eyes looked so tired. He knew she hadn't slept that well in the chair she had used for a bed. He wished he could take away her weariness. But he barely had the energy he needed for himself. He had to share his experience with her before the meds kicked in again and he drifted back to sleep.

"I think I was with God," he shared.

Mark then told her what God had said to him. She asked if he could see what God looked like.

"It wasn't like I was physically there, as if He was standing in front of me or anything. It wasn't like in those movies we've seen where people travel to heaven.

It was just a feeling I had that He spoke to me. I know it happened. I just know it," he shared with her.

"So, what now?" she asked, an exhausted, worried look on her face.

"Can you make some calls for me? See if you can find a priest to stop by? I really want to make confession."

"Of course," Jennifer said, then looked at him intently. "Is there anything else I can do? Or ask other people to do for you?"

Mark thought about it a moment. There was only one thing he could think of.

"Pray," he whispered as he closed his eyes and lay his head back on the pillow. "Just pray."

Jennifer promised she would, and that she would ask others to as well. She then told him how many people had stopped by, the tremendous outpouring of prayers and support from their church. Mark knew that those prayers had helped. He also knew he would need a lot more before he was back to full health again. For the first moment in a long time, he was proud of his faith. He knew he would lean on that faith heavily to get through whatever came next.

Unfortunately, finding a priest on a Saturday morning turned out to be difficult. The first three churches turned down the request saying their priests were too busy with weddings, confession, and baptisms. There wasn't time to stop by. Not just for one person. Mark tried to stay positive, but the desire to release the emotional pain was becoming hard to hold. He knew he wouldn't rest until he got what he needed. Finally, one of Jennifer's friends reached out to a church in a nearby town and found a priest willing to come. She told him that Father Kevin would be there after lunch, which would work out perfectly, since Mark was scheduled be moved from Intensive Care soon.

While Mark waited for Father Kevin, he spent time reflecting, taking inventory of moments in his life he felt most sorry for. He knew the despair he had felt had started in his early twenties, a time when he stopped being involved with church. That was when his life had steadily grown less and less enjoyable. It hadn't happened at once, but slowly, over the course of many years. As disappointments continued to come, he had begun to wonder if he wasn't meant to be happy. The jobs he had lost, the businesses that failed, the growing accumulation of debt. On the outside, he had shrugged it off, told himself and others that he was fine, that he could handle it. In reality, he had been drowning. When Father Kevin arrived, Mark had a litany of sins he needed to be freed from.

"Good afternoon. How are you?" Father Kevin inquired as he entered the room.

"Not so good, Father. I'm recovering from a pretty serious health problem," Mark replied. "By the way, before we start, I want to say I appreciate you coming today. I know you're on your way to a wedding, and I can't tell you how much it means to me that you made time for this. Your church was the fourth one we called."

"Well, I'll admit, when I first got the request, I had to question if I was able to fit it into my schedule or not. Then I considered why God would have brought me your request when I was already pretty busy. After thinking about it like that, I honestly couldn't see any way that I could refuse. God knows what's most important, after all."

"That really means a lot," Mark shared, not sure what to say next. "I almost died Tuesday night, right after I arrived here. The pneumonia I had was so bad that my body started shutting down. They had to sedate me for a couple days. I had machines keeping me alive."

"That's quite a lot to deal with. Can I ask what happened?"

"The doctors said it's related to something I've dealt with for years now. He called it GERD. I guess some of my stomach acid refluxed into my lungs. It was the bacteria that started the pneumonia, and it spread pretty fast," Mark informed him.

"What's GERD? I never heard of it," Father Kevin asked.

"It's an abbreviation for Gastroesophageal Reflux Disease. I've struggled with stomach issues for years. I've been to four, maybe five different doctors and have had every test you can imagine. No one found anything wrong, which is why this is so hard to understand. Normally, I'm a pretty healthy guy. I run, I work out, I take all kinds of weird supplements. And when I say weird, I mean weird. Like ground avocado pits, and diatomaceous earth."

"But you have a diagnosis now, right? That's a good thing then."

"It's not really a diagnosis. It's more like, since I don't have anything else they can find, then the only thing left is IBS or GERD. There's still no real answer yet. I'm just trying to find the right mix of pills to provide me relief. Hopefully what I'm on now will be the help that I've been praying for lately."

"I see. Well, how can I help? What did you call

me here for today?"

"I need you to hear my confession, Father. It's been far too long since I last went, and last night, well, I had a vision. More of an epiphany, I guess."

"Tell me about that," Father Kevin inquired, his eyes becoming soft and gentle.

"I was thinking, during those two days while I was under, it was like I didn't really exist."

"I think I understand what you mean. But you did exist, for the doctors and nurses taking care of you, and for your family who were there by your side."

"I know. But I was no longer in this world. I was somewhere else."

"Where do you think you were?"

"I'm pretty sure it was heaven."

"Really? How can you be sure of that?"

"Well, it wasn't as if I was there walking through the pearly gates, or like I heard choirs of angels or anything. It was more a feeling I had when I was coming off sedation. I remember being told something of great importance."

"Can I ask what that was?"

"I'm pretty sure God told me He didn't want me. At least, not yet. It's like this hospital thing was His way of getting me to realize how fragile my life is. You know, like how quickly it can all pass away. I'm pretty sure it was a reminder, so that I don't waste any more of what time I have left. He told me I had lived a good life so far, but that wasn't what He created me for. He said I was born to live a great life."

"And this made you decide to seek reconciliation?"

"Father, trust me, there have been so many times

in my life that I'm not proud of. So many parts that I wish I could go back and change," Mark tried to explain, choking out the words.

Father Kevin placed one hand on Mark's shoulder. His face bore a look of concern, but his eyes shone with mercy.

"I...I haven't done this for way too long. I can't remember how it starts," Mark admitted. "Plus, I'm still on morphine, so my mind isn't really clear. I'll need you to help."

"That's okay, Mark. God understands. Just tell me what it is you're sorry for."

Mark knew there were prayers he was supposed to say before he asked forgiveness for his sins. But he couldn't remember what they were. His chest began to heave as he fought back tears. Knowing how important this moment was, he fought through, squeezing his eyes tight and tensing his shoulders and jaw until the moment passed. He felt the warmth of Father Kevin's hand on his shoulder. The warmth spread down across his chest and wrapped around his heart, giving him the courage to go on.

"First, I'm sorry I haven't been to church lately. I want to be there, but I haven't been able to leave the house since Christmas last year. The issues related to my IBS have just been too overwhelming. I've missed out on so much this past year, so many memories I will never have. Because I just couldn't be there."

"God understands what you're struggling with, Mark. He forgives you for not being at Mass."

"I'm sorry I gave up on life. I even wanted to end my life a few years ago. Father, I know I'm stronger than that, but I just couldn't carry all this pain. I never want to take my life for granted like that again," Mark struggled to explain, his eyes still shut tight to prevent the tears from falling.

He felt Father Kevin squeeze his shoulder gently, which helped him focus his thoughts.

"I wasn't always there when my children needed me. And I definitely didn't treat my wife with the respect and love she deserves. She is such a good woman. I don't know what I did to deserve her, but I'm definitely blessed. I'm sorry for doubting myself, too, for not taking care of myself the way I should, for not believing in *me*. For so many years I hid in the shadows, never wanting attention, never wanting responsibility. I've passed by far too many opportunities to do the right thing when it really mattered. I was too weak, too frightened."

"God forgives you," Father Kevin whispered.

"There's one more thing, Father. This one I can't believe I did. I challenged the Devil a few years back. Maybe fifteen years now? Maybe more, I don't remember. I told him no matter what he did to me, he couldn't break me. I would never lose my faith. I know I shouldn't have done that. I shouldn't have challenged him that way. I should have put my trust in God to protect me instead. I let my pride get in the way. I believed I could handle him myself. I think that's why my life has been so difficult. I think that's why I've been in so much pain, and why I've been so depressed."

"Pride is one of the most difficult things to overcome," Father Kevin shared. "And you're right, putting your faith in God and trusting that He would give you the strength to face any challenge, well, that would have been the right thing to do. But you're forgiven of that now, too."

Mark had more he wanted to say, but sorrow had overtaken him. He sobbed deeply, his face wet from tears.

"Let's stop there, Mark. God knows what is in your heart. Let it go. He has forgiven you," Father Kevin said, then guided Mark through the Act of Contrition, and then they ended with the prayer of absolution.

Father Kevin paused a moment, then pulled out a vial of oil and blessed Mark with the Anointing of the Sick.

"I think, for the next week, it may be a good idea for you to pray the Chaplet of Divine Mercy. Do you know that prayer?" Father Kevin asked.

"I may have heard it before, but I don't know it by heart," Mark admitted.

Father Kevin pulled out his phone.

"I'll make it easy for you then. All you need to do is download this app," he said, showing Mark his phone. "You can either pray it following the prompts, or put some headphones on and listen to the audio. Do you have your phone here?"

"Yeah, my wife has it right now."

"Okay, good. Ask her to search for *catholic prayer* in the app store when she comes back. You'll find a lot of other resources in there, too," Father Kevin said, the gentle glow returning to his eyes as he smiled at Mark. "I want you to know I'm going to be praying for you as well. I'll ask my congregation to pray for you, too. Both for the healing of your body, and also for peace in your soul. Is there anything else I can do for you while I'm here?"

Mark shook his head.

Father Kevin smiled, this time it was a broad

smile that spread slowly across his face, expanding like a sunrise.

"Be well, Mark. And I expect to see you at Mass soon, okay?"

"I promise," he said, nodding his head and doing his best to smile.

Father Kevin gathered his things and began to depart. Mark felt once more the warmth lingering in his chest. He knew that whatever happened, from this day forth, his life was going to be great. He would make sure it was.

Chapter Two
Struggle

He said to me, "My grace is sufficient for you, for my power is made perfect in weakness." - 2 Corinthians 12:9

Wednesday, October 5

Mark woke with anticipation. His first thought was today he was scheduled to be released from the hospital. Finally he had progressed enough to be granted freedom. He stretched, preparing for his morning trip to the bathroom. As he flexed his left leg, his calf felt firm and tight. He was surprised to discover he couldn't feel his foot as he bent the ankle back and forth. His heart skipped a beat. Something was wrong.

Panicked, he looked to the chair where Jennifer should be sleeping. But she wasn't there. He knew she was most likely at home having a hot meal and a shower. She would be back, he just had no idea when. He was on his own for now. Mark pressed the button that would call his nurse, and then waited for her to arrive. After a couple of minutes passed, he couldn't wait any longer. He would have to get into the bathroom on his own.

He pulled his bedding off and swung his legs over the side, pausing just for a moment to see if there was any pain. There wasn't. So far, that was a good sign. Perhaps his leg had simply fallen asleep. He shifted his weight to the edge of the bed, and then pushed himself up, keeping his weight on his right leg. Carefully, Mark reached forward with his left foot as far as he dared, then shifted his weight to that leg. Pain shot up the leg, making his knee buckle and his mind grow faint. He nearly collapsed. Quickly, he shifted back to the right leg.

"Okay," he whispered through clenched teeth, "this is going to be harder than I thought. At least it's not too far."

With his arms to steady himself, Mark began limping to the bathroom. His hands never let go of whatever support he could find; the bed rail, the arm of a chair, the bathroom door handle. Finally making it into the doorway, he grabbed the metal handicap rail to support him the rest of the way in. As he sat on the toilet, he heard his nurse finally enter the room.

"What do you need, my dear?" she called from near his bed.

"I'm okay for now, but I might need some help getting back. My left leg *really* hurts," he told her. "I can't even stand on it."

"Do you want me to come in? Or bring you anything?" she asked.

"Maybe just some wet washcloths and a new gown."

"Okay, my dear. Let me get them. Do you want me to give you a bath?"

Bath, in hospital talk, meant getting scrubbed with either wet towels or antiseptic wipes. He had already had enough of those. They didn't help him feel any cleaner, though they did control the stink he was brewing. It had been more than a week since his last shower. As long as the central line was inserted in his jugular, the doctors wouldn't let him get wet. How he longed to soak in a warm tub and scour off the weeks' worth of dead skin. It was making him itch. Still, a hospital bath was better than nothing. At least he wouldn't smell for the ride home.

"Okay, sure. Why not?" Mark relented.

She smiled at him from the doorway, and then left the room. Mark liked this nurse. She was by far his favorite of those that had been assigned to him. He liked how she called him 'my dear'. Even if it was just a phrase. It made him feel comfortable, as if he belonged. He would miss having her take care of him. Yet even that wasn't enough to have him stay any longer. Hopefully whatever was going on with his leg wouldn't either. He wanted nothing more than to escape these walls.

His nurse returned, tapped on the door, and asked if it was okay to enter. He told her it was. She set two wet washcloths on the edge of the sink, and then proceeded to scrub him with a third. The cloths weren't very warm, which left Mark shivering slightly. She handed him a clean gown, helping him drape it over his head. It provided little relief from the chill. That left him only one option. Get back in bed.

"You're going to have to help me walk," he told his nurse. "I can't put any weight on my left leg. I don't know what's wrong, but it feels really tight, like someone kicked me in the calf."

"Let me take a look," she said, tossing the wash cloths and his old gown in a hamper.

Mark stretched his legs out in front of him. The left one was almost twice the size of the right.

"My dear!" she exclaimed. "Your leg is so

swollen! Have they checked you for blood clots?"

"No, I don't think so. Not since I've been awake, at least."

"Let's get you into bed, then I'll schedule an ultrasound. We can't let you leave if you're not able to walk," she informed him.

An hour later, Jennifer arrived. He explained what was going on with his leg, and what his nurse thought it might be. She told him how the doctor in the ICU had warned about the possibility of a clot. She also said they had been changing his position every hour, and that he had been on blood thinners from the moment he had been sedated, so she hoped it was something else. Mark informed her about the ultrasound test, and that they would find out soon enough.

Jennifer then spent a few moments bringing him up to date on what was happening at home. She even gave a detailed report on the latest adventures of their cats. Just before lunch a nurse arrived to transport him for his ultrasound. It was the first time he had been out of his private room, other than walking with the physical therapist. But that was just around the nurses' station and back.

Jennifer came with him, as she had quite a few questions she wanted to ask. The technician who performed the ultrasound stated she wasn't qualified to read the test, only to perform it. They would have to wait for Mark's doctor before knowing if anything was wrong. Mark could tell his wife was far more concerned than she was letting on.

After the ultrasound, the transport nurse brought him back to his room. There, they waited again, this time for his doctor to bring the results. Mark knew patients were usually released between eleven o'clock and three. It was now almost half-past two. If they didn't start his discharge soon, he would wind up staying one more night, even if there was no clot. That was something he simply didn't want to happen. He began to ask Jennifer every five minutes to check on where the doctor might be. He was now as anxious as she had been during the test.

When his doctor did arrive, it was to give him the news he had hoped he wouldn't hear. They had found not just one clot, but two, large clots. One was located in his calf, and the other in his thigh. The doctor explained what this new information meant. The clots would require additional medication and therapy. Unfortunately, it also meant at least one more night of observation.

Mark was crestfallen. He wanted nothing more than to be in his own bed, sit on his own couch, and watch his own television. Things he usually took for granted never held such strong attraction. Most of all, he craved real food. He had rejected every meal they had brought. Everything not only smelled the same, but tasted the same as well. How they were able to make chicken, fish, pork, beef, and eggs that all tasted the same, he couldn't understand. He was surviving on Greek yogurt and fruit. He had already lost fifteen pounds.

On a positive note, Mark had also lost most of the wires that had been chaining him to his bed. At least he had gained that much freedom. Although it had come with some cost. Since he no longer needed to be monitored, they were going to transfer him to a semi-private room on another floor. This meant leaving behind the nursing staff he had come to know. It also meant Jennifer would not be allowed to stay with him overnight. Mark dreaded spending the night alone. He was uncomfortable being left with just his thoughts. They had betrayed him so many times.

While he waited for the transport team to move him once more, Mark lay in bed, thumbing randomly on his phone. He wanted to pray, but he had never learned anything more than a few simple prayers. He thought he might find an app that would help. In his search, he came across one that would allow him to post a prayer request and let other people pray for him. Mark loaded the app, set up an account, and then submitted his request. He asked for prayers for his health, successful recovery from his blood clots, and for protection from any other medical concerns. Within a few moments, his request garnered dozens of responses.

Though most were quick replies letting him know he was being prayed for, one response caught his eye. It suggested he pray a novena to St. Theresa. She said when she had prayed the novena, on the third day she had been granted a miracle. She knew the miracle was coming because she had been given a rose. This, she knew, was as a sign from St. Theresa that her prayers had been heard.

Mark researched to find out more about this saint and the gift of roses she provided. He learned her nickname was *The Little Flower*, and that she had died at a fairly young age. Since he didn't know many of the other saints, he decided it couldn't hurt praying to this one. He found the prayers and said the one for the first day, and then waited. Nothing changed. Not sure he had done the prayers correctly, Mark went back to thumbing aimlessly on his phone. He read a few Facebook updates from his friends and then played an online game. Finally, the transport team arrived.

On the way to his new room they passed by a bank of windows that appeared to provide a view outside the hospital. Until now, Mark only had a small, semi-obscured view from the narrow window in the corner of his room. He hadn't seen a plant or animal in more than a week. Longing to be in the outdoors once more, a place where he always felt more at peace, Mark grew excited as they drew closer to the windows. If he couldn't go outside, then at least he could hold in his memory the images he would soon see.

When they reached the windows, he realized they didn't provide a view of the outside world, but of an atrium. On each side of the atrium, Mark could see other areas of the hospital. Directly across from him was a small boy, perhaps four or five years old. The boy was pressing his nose up against the window and licking the glass. They stared at each other for a moment, then the boy was gone, dragged off by his mom to wherever it is young boys get dragged off to.

Although the view wasn't what he hoped, there were still plants and a few birds that Mark could see. He looked longingly at the two Japanese maple trees, the small water fountain, and the dozen or so tiny plants that lived within the four walls. Trapped inside their prison, the sad, lonely flora reached out to Mark as if they envied his freedom.

"If only they knew the truth," Mark thought, taking a moment to consider each plant in turn.

The plants held only a smattering of foliage on thin branches that drooped sorrowfully. He could find no blossoms. They simply didn't have the strength to bloom. That is, all but one. On the final bush Mark viewed, a tiny flicker of red peeked out through the sepals.

It was a rose!

A rush of good emotions flooded through him, willing his heart to follow.

"She heard me!" Mark whispered excitedly.

"Who heard you?" Jennifer inquired.

Mark hadn't realized he had spoken out loud.

"Oh, nothing, hon," he fibbed, too embarrassed to share the truth. "I was just daydreaming."

Jennifer made a *humph* sound, and gave him a look that said she would ask her question again when they were in private. Mark smiled slyly back at her. She winked at him playfully, and then turned away.

The transport team navigated Mark's bed to the left, and they entered yet another ordinary, cold, neutral-toned hallway. The atrium disappeared from view, but Mark had the memory of the vision stuck firmly in his mind.

"Thank you, Saint Theresa, for the gift of your flower," Mark thought, this time ensuring his thoughts remained just thoughts.

The tiny parade stopped at a nursing station.

"Which room do you want the bed?" one of the transport team asked.

"Put it in 117, on the 'A' side," the nurse said from behind the protective wall of her station.

Mark frowned. He wasn't *Mark* to these nurses. He definitely wasn't 'my dear'. He wasn't even a person. He was just a package. His bed was just the box. Oh, how he craved the moment he would leave this place.

The bed moved once more, making one final turn down yet another hallway, then it swung to the left as they entered a room. Mark could tell by the foul odor that the meal cart was somewhere close by. His stomach turned.

"Jennifer?" he said, his face scrunched in a look of disgust.

"Yeah?" she replied, as she set up his bed tray with everything he would need.

"Don't let them bring one of those meals in here. I don't want to even smell it."

"Are you sure? You really need to get your strength back. You're looking so thin!"

"Then just a sandwich. Peanut butter or something," he replied.

"Okay. Let me go tell them now," Jennifer said, giving him one last worried glance before heading towards the door.

Mark watched as she left, then looked around his new room. It was much larger than the private room he had just left, with updated furniture and décor. Instead of the plain, light-gray tile floor, this room had dark walnut, hardwood laminate. The walls were painted a light shade of blue, giving the illusion that the room was even larger than it was. His bed had been placed on the left half of the room, with his feet towards the center. Across from him, in the other half of the room, an empty bed sat against the wall.

There were curtains hanging from several different tracks, allowing the room to be divided into two equal spaces. Though the curtains provided some visual privacy, there was no way they would conceal sound. Should another patient be assigned to this room, they would be able to hear everything Mark and Jennifer said. That was okay with Mark. He didn't feel much like talking right now anyway. He was done sharing his thoughts, tired of answering the countless *'how are you'* inquiries. Maybe being alone for a while was what he needed.

It was a strange duality wanting to be alone and yet dreading being exactly that. Alone. Mark sighed deeply, turning to the one activity he had some control over, choosing which television channel to watch. He lay there in his bed, in this new, mostly empty room, absentmindedly flipping through the stations, while tears filled his eyes. Eventually, he gave up changing channels, giving way to the sadness. He tossed the remote to the floor, burying his face in his pillow.

"This isn't how this day was supposed to end," Mark thought as tears continued to fall. *"This isn't how it was supposed to end."*

Thursday, October 6

Finally, on the morning of his tenth day, he got the news he had been waiting for. He would be released! The moment couldn't come soon enough. There were a few last items that would need to be complete before he could be discharged. Mark grew more and more anxious as the minutes ticked by. The only distraction being the constant parade of hospital staff who came through to see him. The first to arrive was the doctor who had taken care of him in the Intensive Care unit. He shared with Mark how grateful he was that Mark had survived, explaining once more how close it had been. His previous nurses stopped by as well, happy to see that

Mark was doing so much better.

The final visitor was the one Mark had been wanting for six days now. A nurse arrived to remove the IV line from his jugular. Having that needle sticking into his neck, especially while taking blood thinner medication, had kept Mark in a constant state of nervousness. He had had dreams in which he accidentally ripped the line out, watching in horror as his life blood poured out, the world around him fading away. As she cut the sutures holding the line, Mark was tense. His hands curled into tight fists, his breathing becoming short and abrupt. Finally, it was out.

Mark's entire body relaxed as his mind let go of the fear that had gripped him for nearly a week. Finally, nothing remained but a wheelchair ride to the front door. Jennifer had run ahead to move the car, and she was already waiting for him at the curb. He was free. Totally free. Physically, he was free of the encumbrances of the hospital. Spiritually, he was free from the weight of his sins. Mentally, he was free to begin transforming his life from one of 'good enough' to one of greatness.

Friday, October 14

Back at home, the first thing Mark had to do was recover, which took longer than expected. The pain in his leg had taken a week to subside. Walking was still difficult, but he was learning. Jennifer had rented him a walker, which he used the first three days. As the pain subsided, he moved from the walker to a cane. Today was the first day he could walk on his own. Finally, he was able to go outside and enjoy his backyard.

Walking through the serene retreat gave him a

tremendous sense of pride. These were the trees he had planted. This was the deck he had built. When they had started remodeling their yard, it had been nothing more than bare ground. Together, they had created a relaxing oasis. If they could accomplish that, Mark considered, then how much more could they do?

Suddenly, Mark understood that his journey to his 'great' life was not one he would take on his own. His wife would play a large role, as she had since the day they met. He knew he was the man he was because of the tremendous support Jennifer always gave. He had admitted to himself several times over the years that, had it not been for Jennifer, he would never have learned how to love, or how to be loved. Most of the personal growth he had achieved in the thirty-two years they had been together was due to the patience and unconditional acceptance she provided him.

Sure, there were days when one or the other would get in a foul mood, or they would argue about something that was, in all honesty, completely trivial. But that was just part of being in a long-term relationship. There would always be good days, and there would always be not-so-good days. He knew they couldn't make it work by constantly trying to be happy. Life wasn't built for that, and marriages aren't either. Instead, the trick was accepting that neither are perfect. To learn to love the other person, not in spite of their flaws, but because of them.

As he slowly wound his way past an apple tree, Mark had another revelation. The tree he was walking past was losing its leaves. Fall was quickly moving towards winter. His garden would once more be bare. He understood that this, too, was part of the process of life. There could be no life without death, no gain without loss, no joy without sorrow. To appreciate what he perceived as the good parts of life, he had to accept the parts he didn't like as well. How could he ever experience the pleasure of sitting on his deck, in the shade of one of his trees, enjoying the lingering moments of a warm, summer day if he never felt the bitter cold of winter?

Perhaps, Mark considered, the key to having a great life was not to be found in a collection of things, but rather in the accumulation of love. The physical objects and wealth he previously sought, believing they held the key to the life he desired, had brought him only fleeting moments of joy. When the luster of his new purchases wore off, so did the peace and satisfaction those purchases brought. This left him scratching his head and wondering if he would ever find true happiness.

And yet, that which he desired had been with him all along. All he had to do was to accept life as it came, taking the good days with the bad. He understood that, in some way, had he not come so close to death just a few weeks ago, he may never have reached this new understanding. What he had at first considered to be a negative experience, a troubling and painful part of his life, had in fact given him one of the greatest gifts he had ever known. If that was true, then Mark couldn't regret the time he had spent in the hospital.

Mark began to look at other parts of his life, parts that he had at once thought of as painful or sad. For each of those moments, he could also recall a moment of joy, a moment that wouldn't have been as bright if he hadn't first experienced the sorrow.

He recalled the time when a good friend had passed away, which had left Mark feeling depressed and angry for days. Yet, at the funeral, he bumped into a high school classmate with whom he had lost touch over the years. That renewed friendship was something Mark valued even today. He thought about the businesses he had started, only to see them fail. Even still, he knew that the lessons he learned through the process of shutting those businesses down had given him the courage to take on even bigger challenges.

Mark realized that life wasn't good or bad because good or bad things happened, it was good or bad because he chose it to be that way. Sure, there were instances that felt more difficult, or moments when his patience or perseverance were tested, but those were only considered negative or bad because Mark had chosen for them to be so. Life wasn't good, and it wasn't bad. Life wasn't anything at all, at least until Mark decided what it was.

This, then, must be the key to transforming from a good life to a great one. This had to be the way he would become the person he was born to be. At that moment, Mark's foot caught on the edge of a stepping stone, causing him to stumble and fall. He landed in the middle of a lantana bush. His left leg screamed as he struggled to free himself from the branches. Small red lines on his face and arms grew as tiny scratches bled.

Mark felt anger boiling inside, which was his usual response whenever something unexpected happened, whenever something bad... He paused, his mind locked on the realization that he was about to consider this moment as being 'bad'. Rolling onto his back, Mark looked up at the sky and gazed at the clouds casually drifting past. He heard Jennifer rushing over to help. She stood over him, an anxious look on her face, with the sun behind her, creating a halo of light.

"She looks like an angel," Mark thought with a smile.

Seeing his smile, Jennifer's face changed from anxious to curious. Eventually she smiled too. Mark reached up to her. Believing he needed her help standing up, she took his hands in hers. Instead, he pulled her down on top of him. Jennifer gasped. Pushing up slightly, she looked at her husband, feeling a bit shocked. Mark was grinning from ear to ear. There was a twinkle in his eyes.

"What are you doing, weirdo?" Jennifer teased.

"Testing a theory," Mark replied, giving her a playful smile.

"And?" she inquired, a smile starting to grow wide and playful.

"I'll tell you all about it. For now, let's get out of this lantana. I'm starting to itch."

They helped each other up, then grabbed a seat in their matching lounge chairs on the deck. It was warm outside, but not so warm they couldn't sit in the full light of the sun.

"So, what's going on?" Jennifer asked, her eyes reflecting a small level of concern.

Mark thought for a moment, considering how best to explain his recent revelations. It had been quite a long time since he had been completely honest and open with anyone, his wife included. Perhaps it was a defense mechanism carried over from his youth, something he had relied on to feel safe. He wasn't purposefully hiding something, he just had a difficult time revealing his true thoughts and feelings. It was simply something Mark did, even though he didn't quite understand why.

His inability to be open and honest had left Jennifer confused more than once, which had caused some tension in their marriage. Yet, just as he had held onto his sins for far too many years, Mark had also held onto his fear of being vulnerable. He never considered that if he let his wife know his true thoughts, it might provide him the peace he had been searching for most of his life.

"I'm not sure how to explain it," he began, taking a pause to structure his thoughts in a logical sequence. "You know I was born Catholic, raised in the church my whole life. I received every sacrament I was supposed to, all at an age when I really didn't understand what was going on. Even when I was confirmed, I didn't really understand the meaning and purpose of that event.

"Back then, they were still confirming kids in the seventh or eighth grade. In fact, I only have two memories of that time. The first was when they took us to that retreat center. You know, the one behind the cemetery? I don't remember what we did, or who all was there. I just remember sitting in that big room, the one with the fireplace.

"Anyhow, the other memory is the day of my confirmation. I was so nervous before the Bishop. I was afraid I would forget what I was supposed to say. I was afraid he wouldn't confirm me for some reason. I have no idea why I had those fears, but I did."

Mark took a deep breath, calming the anxiousness in his heart. Jennifer sat in silence, allowing him the time and space to share what he needed in his own way. She always had great patience. It was part of what made her such a great teacher.

"But then," Mark continued, "after we got confirmed, there wasn't anything for us teenagers to do. Other than being altar servers or singing with one of the youth choirs. Teens didn't have a chance to participate in the Mass back then, not like they do now. The church did have a volunteer who ran a youth group, but it was mostly a social gathering. We just hung out, made a lot of noise, and played street hockey. They didn't have any religion classes or bible study groups for kids that age. If we wanted to participate in something, we were told to join one of the adult groups.

"But then we got a new group of priests assigned to our church, and things began to change. One of the Associate Pastors formed a new youth group. Again, it was more social than social justice, but we did get involved as best as we could. We had our own very limited budget, just enough to buy cookies and punch. We were responsible for raising our own money if we wanted to do anything big. So we held car washes and dances, even had a lock-in. Not quite the same as they are doing now, but we did have some small group sessions and listened to a couple people talk about their faith. It wasn't anything that helped me understand *my* faith though."

Mark paused. He knew he was rambling a bit. This wasn't the real conversation he wanted to have. He thought that perhaps if he just kept talking, the parts he wanted to share would somehow leak out too. But that wasn't fair to Jennifer. He could tell she was already confused where this conversation was going. There was really only one way to explain.

"Sorry, babe. I think I've been rambling a bit. Let

me start again," he admitted. "You know how the front of the church bulletin shows the church's mission? You know, the whole 'Know Christ better and make Him better known' thing? Well, I don't think I've done either one of those very well, if at all. I mean, we go to church, most weekends, when it's convenient for us and we don't have any other plans. And we've done the Marriage Encounter retreat, and a few other retreats too. But how well do we really know Jesus? I don't know, maybe you feel you have a better understanding or relationship with Him than I do.

"And the part about 'making Him better known.' Have we done anything to do that? Sure, we have a few friends at church, and we get together with them once or twice a year outside of Mass. But that's all pretty superficial, don't you think? I mean, if we are supposed to make Him better known, shouldn't we be spending more time talking about Him? Even if only between ourselves?"

Mark turned to look at his wife. Although she was absentmindedly picking at her nail polish, he knew that was just how she processed. Jennifer was an active learner. She didn't absorb information through reading or listening, but by doing. Mark learned that about her on one of the retreats they had attended. It took another few seconds for her to lift her eyes to meet his.

"I hear what you're saying," she began. "It's something I thought about recently, too. Especially when I was sitting in the ICU with nothing to do but pray. I suddenly became aware that my prayer life wasn't as strong as I thought. I didn't know any of the standard prayers, outside of the Our Father and Hail Mary, and I've never been good at finding the right words to just pray on my own.

"Most of the time I just held my rosary beads and cried. Somehow I had this feeling God knew what it was that I wanted to say, even though I couldn't figure it out for myself. Maybe I don't really know him that well, because it didn't feel like I was talking to someone I've known for almost thirty years."

Jennifer had been born and raised Catholic, but, unlike her husband, she was never really involved in church as a teen. She had never felt comfortable with her faith and had far more questions than Mark had answers for when they first met. Over the years, she had taken time to learn everything she could, but there was still quite a bit she wasn't aware of. But it really wasn't until she started volunteering with a local church after their oldest child had been born that her true relationship with God had begun, which is why she felt as if she had only really been Catholic since they were married.

"I know what you mean, Jen. Sometimes I think my prayer life is more like going to a vending machine than real prayer. I pray when I'm stressed, or when something isn't going the way I want. It's like I only turn to God when I need something. Yet, when I feel that He wants something from me, I turn away and pretend that I didn't hear Him.

"I think that all changed in the hospital. At least, I would like to think that it is changing. I want to change, but I'm just not sure how."

The afternoon sun drifted slowly towards the horizon. The world around them was filled with the sounds of birds chirping, leaves rustling and neighborhood children at play. The warmth of the sun and the cool, early fall breeze had a peaceful feel to them.

As his mind drifted towards slumber, a new thought floated casually by. He had been given a gift. What that gift was, and what it was for, he had yet to understand.

Chapter Three
Discovery

It is the glory of God to conceal things, but the glory of kings is to search things out - Proverbs 25:2

Sunday, October 16

Mark woke slowly, his eyes not quite ready to open, his mind not yet ready to engage. He could hear that Jennifer was already awake, busy with something in the kitchen. Slowly, he rolled over, wrapping himself even tighter inside the covers. He considered staying that way, at least for the day. But he had made a promise, to himself and to Father Kevin. A promise he had no desire to break. Mark glanced at the clock. It was just after eight. Mass would begin in less than two hours. But, to ensure he was able to find a seat, he would have to arrive at least fifteen minutes before that. There was no way he would be able to stand for the entire service, not while he was still dealing with the pain in his leg and the lingering weakness in his body.

Recovery was only creeping back in. His back ached. His hips and knees hurt, too. Even his shoulders were letting him know they weren't very happy with him this morning. Mark feared it would be quite the process just getting up, let alone getting ready.

Of course, they could attend the youth mass in the evening. He had been to that one a few times. It wasn't as heavily attended, so there should be no

41

concern finding a seat. He liked the music at that Mass more than at the morning one. The band leader for the group was willing to try newer material, whereas the Sunday morning choir was still singing the same songs Mark had learned thirty years ago. The only concern in waiting for the later service was whether or not Father Kevin would be there.

Mark considered the promise he had made. He realized he hadn't said that he would see Father Kevin, but that Father Kevin would see him. That meant, it didn't matter which Mass he attended. As long as he was there, Mark knew he was honoring his part of the bargain. He reached for his phone and sent his wife a quick text message to let her know that he didn't feel well enough to attend the morning services and that they should try for the evening one instead. Then he placed his phone on the nightstand and went back to sleep.

Dreams came slowly at first, opening in tiny fragments. The first thing his subconscious mind connected with, was cold. Wherever he was in this dream, it was bitter cold. Not just physically, but emotionally, too. The air bit harshly. His lungs ached. Mark wondered if this was what it felt like to die. He didn't recall feeling anything those first few days in the hospital. But he hadn't died then. He had only come close to dying.

Turning his head to see what was around him, Mark sensed a familiarity to his surroundings, as if he had been here before. The limited light that filtered in through an almost opaque window above his head gave just enough illumination for him to make out what had to be a wall. Even in the dim lighting, Mark could make out the standard running pattern of concrete blocks.

Their usual dull gray looked even more colorless in the shadows.

Continuing to turn, Mark spotted what had to be the handrail. The upward slope was consistent with the angle of a stairway. Moving that direction, his eyes picked out a few additional details, proving his first observation was correct. Stairs headed up, giving Mark hope that he might find a way out, hopefully into warmer climes. Pausing at the first step, his hand gently caressed the rail. There was definitely something familiar about it. He began to climb, pausing after each step to listen for any sounds from above.

Hearing nothing but the silent whispers of his own heartbeat, Mark continued his ascent. On the fifth step, the boards creaked and shifted in a way that caught his attention. He stepped back down, and then climbed up once more. The creaking of the step called to him, urging his mind to connect the fleeting memory. Nothing came.

Onward he climbed. Ten, eleven, twelve steps up. A thin yellow-white line gradually came into view. It rose from about the height of his waist, up until it was over his head, took a ninety-degree turn to the right, traveled another short distance, and then turned ninety degrees again, this time heading back downward.

"It's the outline of a door!" Mark thought, wondering again where he was.

Calculating where the bottom of the outline began, Mark estimated that there were only two steps left, maybe three, before he would reach the top. His mind raced, wondering if it would be locked, curious as to what might be on the other side, and questioning if he was brave enough to find out. Mark took the next two steps with great caution, his senses on full alert. He could feel his ears pull back, opening more fully as they searched the silence. His nostrils flared as well, testing for familiar smells. The hairs on his arms stood upright, reaching into the black void.

Mark tested the darkness with his right foot, gently inching it forward until it hit something solid. He raised his foot slowly, dragging along the obstruction, checking its height. When his foot lifted further than the height of one of the steps, he knew he had reached the landing. The obstruction before him had to be the door.

He reached out his hand until it contacted the door. He felt a rough veneer, telling him the door was made of wood. It felt warm, much warmer than the air surrounding him. He slid his fingers towards the thin line of light, then downward, searching for a handle. Something cool and smooth touched his fingers. He wrapped his hand around it, praying it wouldn't be locked.

Carefully, as slowly as he could, Mark turned the knob. The deadlatch creaked softly. He paused, once again focusing his senses, seeking any indication of what might be waiting for him on the other side. Nothing registered. Mark twisted the handle further. His heart raced. The spindle made a scraping noise as it drew the latch inside, the door opening just a crack. A warm breeze washed over his hand and arm. Mark wondered if he should go back down and search the room below for clues as to what might be waiting on the other side. Curiosity urged him forward. He pushed the door inward. Light filled the growing crack. His eyes adjusted slowly, allowing him to see details that had been hidden before. The door was wood, his fingers hadn't lied.

Glancing down, he looked at the knob he was holding. It was a bell shaped knob, made from a yellow-colored metal, most likely brass. Most of the handle was covered in a green patina showing its age. The door was probably just as old, as were the stairs he had just climbed.

Suddenly, something caught his attention. A familiar smell drifted in, sneaking its way through the crack. Mark breathed deep, recognizing the smell. *Halupki!* He knew there was only one person who could make stuffed cabbage rolls that smelled this good. He began to feel safe, releasing his anxiousness as old memories flooded in.

The room where the dream had started was the basement of his grandparents' house. It was cold because it was underground. Even in the summer months, when it was hot enough to fry eggs on the street, the basement was always cool. In the winter, it was frigid.

At the top of the stairs was a door, this same one he now held slightly ajar. On the other side he would find a small landing. Directly opposite of the door he was holding there would be another door, this one leading outside. To the left would be a small kitchen. Mark hadn't been inside that kitchen since he was twelve. As he pushed the door open more fully, he was struck by just how small the kitchen was. Far smaller than he remembered.

He wondered if he would find the rest of the house to be just as small. To be truthful, there wasn't much more to see. A modest living room, one tiny bathroom, and two small bedrooms. The entire house was under one thousand square feet. Barely enough space for his grandparents. Nowhere near enough room for them to have raised eight children. Yet that was exactly what they had done. Mark leaned closer, turned his head to the side, and placed his left ear near the door. Still nothing registered. If there was someone home, they weren't making any noise. He twisted his body, trying to see as much as he could of the room beyond. Satisfied that no one was there, he opened the door far enough to let himself pass through, pausing just once more as he took in the scene before him.

Other than the standard furniture one might find in a kitchen which, in this case, included a small table and three chairs, the room was empty. Pausing to look at the table, Mark saw it had been set for two. The plates and silverware were perfectly placed, the water glasses filled to the exact same height. A small vase held three flowers that looked so fresh they must have just been cut. No food was on the table yet. A loaf of bread, still in its pan, was cooling on the cutting board. A single pot was on the stove, steam escaping through the slightly tilted lid. Mark's stomach rumbled. He found it odd that he was able to sense hunger in the middle of a dream.

A rustling sound caught his attention. Mark moved cautiously towards the doorway leading into the living room, taking a position with his back against the wall. Leaning slightly and twisting his neck, he peeked around the corner. The room was furnished sparingly, with a small television on a stand against one wall, two comfortable chairs against another, and a long couch along the wall to his left. Sitting on the couch, a newspaper in his hand, was an older gentleman Mark recognized right away.

"Grandpa?" Mark asked, moving into the room. "What are you doing here?"

He realized it was an odd question. After all, the

house he was in belonged to the man on the couch. He waited as his grandfather bent the corner of the newspaper, peering over the top to see who was there. A smile found its way to his grandfather's face, his eyes lighting up with joy.

"Well, there's the troublemaker! I've been wondering when you would arrive. Where have you been?" his grandfather inquired.

As a child, Mark had gotten into trouble just about every time his visited his grandparents. It hadn't taken long for him to receive that nickname. He glanced at the corner of the room between the couch and the chairs. This was the corner he had been assigned to for his punishments. Typically, the punishment was nothing more than losing out on something fun the rest of his siblings were doing, while he sat there staring at the wallpaper. At times, when his offense was more egregious, he had felt the end of a belt on his backside first.

"I'm not sure, Grandpa. I think I might be dreaming, though. I didn't think I would see you…"

Mark had been about to say 'again'. But, still unsure if he was in a dream or not, he had caught himself. From what he remembered, his grandfather had died almost seven years ago.

"Well, grab a seat. I think dinner is almost ready. Maybe I can finally eat tonight."

Mark wondered what his grandfather meant by that remark. He walked across the room, choosing the chair closest to the couch. It was the one he was always drawn to as a child. This was the chair where his grandmother always sat. He knew that if he was in it when she wanted to sit, she would coax him out with the offer of a cookie or two. He felt a pang of sadness as he remembered his grandparents. His grandmother had passed away first, about ten years ago. That loss had hit him pretty hard. It had hit his grandfather even harder.

"Is Grandma here too?" he wondered aloud.

Grandpa carefully folded the newspaper and set it to the side. Mark could see that the question had brought a tear to his eye.

"No. She didn't come to this place. She went straight to heaven," Grandpa explained, releasing a long, sorrowful sigh. "She loved her faith deeply, you know."

Mark could agree with that. He had learned most of what he now knew about his faith from his grandmother. Most often, when she took a moment to rest from the constant cooking and cleaning that kept her busy, his grandmother would take a seat, open her well-worn bible, and read scriptures. She had taught Mark how to pray, talked to him about the Gospel, and had shared her favorite bible stories again and again. Mark loved sitting on her lap as she told him of her love for Jesus.

"Then, who made the dinner?" Mark asked, suddenly aware that he had never seen his grandfather in the kitchen other than at mealtimes.

"I don't know. It's always like this for me. I sit here on this couch, reading this same newspaper, smelling the halupki. It's always almost ready, but somehow never is."

Mark wondered at the words he just heard. Was his grandfather telling the truth? By the sullen look on his grandfather's face, Mark considered that what he had just heard had to be true.

"But come, that's not why you're here. I've been

asked to help you understand the questions racing around in that inquisitive mind of yours. You always were the curious one. Taking apart whatever you could get your hands on to see how things worked, experimenting," Grandpa said as a half-smile crept over his face. "But this time there's nothing to take apart. Even if you did, it wouldn't help you understand. We're talking about life here, not some mechanical device or gadget."

"I don't understand, Grandpa."

Grandpa folded his hands in his lap, shifting his position to face Mark more fully.

"Your mind is filled with questions. You want to understand why you got so sick. You want to understand the words God spoke to you. You're trying to figure out what you're supposed to do, but you can't figure it out that way.

"Let me ask you this. If you were lost in the woods, could you figure out where you were going by looking at the footprints you left behind?" Grandpa inquired.

"Probably not. Not looking at each footprint individually, no," Mark admitted. "I would need a lot more than that."

"Exactly. Yet that's what you're trying to do now. You're looking at your current situation as if it holds the answer to everything in life. But it's only one footprint. It doesn't help you understand where you've been, and it sure as heck isn't going to help you understand where you're going."

"So, what am I supposed to do?" Mark asked, obviously befuddled.

"What would you do if you really were lost in the

woods?" Grandpa asked, crossing his arms against his chest and looking at Mark over the top of his glasses.

"Well, I wouldn't just wander aimlessly, that's for sure. I'd try to find a higher vantage point, try to see as much of the area around me as I could. I might try to figure out the direction I had been walking. And I'd probably take some time to find shelter or food. And definitely water."

Grandpa nodded, a single 'huff' the only sound he made. Mark waited for a response, his mind searching to see if he left something out.

"Oh, yeah. I would also try to remember why I was in the woods in the first place. Did I come out here to take a walk? Was I searching for something? Did I wind up out here accidentally? Yeah, I'd try to figure out why I was in the woods."

This time, Grandpa smiled his half-smile again, his eyes shining once more as he did.

"So? What does that tell you about your current situation, and what you're currently doing to figure things out?" he asked.

Mark pondered the question. He honestly had no idea how to answer.

"Don't get lost in the woods?" Mark asked tentatively.

"Too late. You're already there. In fact, you've been there most of your life. But you already knew that, didn't you," Grandpa shared.

This time, Mark understood. For most of his life, he had felt lost, unsure where he was going, not certain how he had come to be wherever it was that he was. And, as Grandpa had put it, all he had ever done was look at the last few footprints left behind, hoping that they would hold the answers to the questions in his mind. But they never did.

"I think I understand, Grandpa. My life has been like the woods, and I have felt lost, desperately lost at times. And, like I did as a child, I'm trying to find something to take apart so that I can understand how things work. But I'm only looking at the last few months in time, maybe a year or two at most.

"I need to find higher ground. I need to get a look at what's around me. I need to see if there are any landmarks I recognize, see if I can tell where the woods began, or where they might end. I need to see the whole picture, not just the individual parts."

"And just how do you think you do that?" Grandpa inquired, urging Mark to explore his thoughts further.

"I don't know," Mark admitted.

"Think about it a little more. It will come. You've always been a smart one. Figure it out. The chair you're sitting in should give you a clue."

Mark put his hands on the armrests of the chair, rubbing them slightly like Grandma used to do. Looking to his left, he saw Grandma's bible on the small table next to the lamp. On top of the bible he saw her rosary beads. The pale blue beads glinted faintly as he reached for them.

"Grandma always said that when you don't know where to go, ask Mary," he whispered, his fingers caressing the smooth glass beads.

"She always did have a strong faith," Grandpa said wistfully. "But there's one thing you probably never knew about your grandmother. Even with all her prayers and scriptures and going to church every day, she never really felt that she knew Jesus, not how she wanted. She always felt there was something more she should be doing.

"Faith isn't about knowing that everything is right, or perfect, or good. It's about believing it is. She taught me that. I only wish I had understood much earlier in my life. Maybe I wouldn't be stuck here reading this newspaper, constantly waiting for dinner to be served. Maybe I'd be with her," Grandpa said, his voice tight as he fought back tears. "I don't want the same to happen to you, Mark. Please, don't make the mistakes I made. Don't think you are strong enough to handle life on your own, that you can find your own way out of that damned forest. Find the higher ground, Mark. Always seek the higher ground!"

Suddenly, Mark understood. His grandfather wasn't in heaven. He wasn't in hell either. He was stuck somewhere in between. Mark knew his grandfather had lived a good life. He was a generous man who was always helping his family, friends, and neighbors whenever he could. But he wasn't a devoted Catholic. He rarely went to church with Grandma, and never during the week. When he did go, there had to be no football or baseball games that he would miss, no chores that needed to get done. Grandpa always made an excuse for not going. Mark suddenly realized he had been doing the same thing the past few years.

Mark stood, sensing that their time was coming to an end. He walked over, sitting beside his grandfather, taking the man's frail hands in his own. He waited until Grandpa raised his eyes to meet his gaze.

"Grandpa, I promise you, I will do what you ask. I'll find the higher ground. I will figure out what my purpose in life is, the reason I'm out there in those woods," Mark said, gently stroking Grandpa's hands. "And I'll pray for you as well. Grandma always said our prayers can help others get to heaven, those that have lost their way. I promise you I'll do my best to help you get back to Grandma."

Grandpa pulled his hands away, stretching his arms out and wrapping them around his grandson. Mark returned the embrace, holding on to the man he had loved so dearly as a child. Together, they cried for opportunities lost, for the failure to understand how much strength could be found in admitting when they were weak. When they had shed every tear they could, Grandpa released his embrace, sitting back far enough to look Mark in the eye. He held that gaze for a moment, and then looked away.

"It's time for you to go now. You'll find the way out back down in the cellar. Make sure to close the door behind you when you leave," Grandpa said, turning his attention back to his newspaper. "I don't want a draft."

Mark pushed the newspaper aside and reached over to give his grandfather one last hug, and then stood up. He made his way back towards the kitchen, each step feeling heavier than the last. He knew now what he needed to do, both for his own sake and for the sake of his grandfather's soul. As he was about to cross the threshold into the kitchen, he turned to look at Grandpa one last time, but he was hidden once more behind his paper. Mark turned to leave.

"Oh, Mark? Can you check the timer on the stove for me? Let me know how many minutes are left." Grandpa requested.

Mark walked to the small oven. He had to squint

slightly to see through the fogged glass.

"It looks like there are ten minutes left."

"Yeah." Grandpa sighed, "There's always ten minutes left."

Chapter Four
Understanding

Trust in the Lord with all your heart, and do not lean on your own understanding - Proverbs 3:5

Sunday, November 6

Three weeks had passed since Mark's dream. Upon waking after the dream, he had spent the day in silence, forgoing his standard football and snacking. Instead, he had had breakfast, made a large cup of tea, and had gone out back to reflect. There, he had pondered the meaning of the dream, seeking clues as to its message. Though he understood the analogy of the forest in relation to his own life, he still hadn't been sure where he was supposed to find this 'higher ground' Grandpa had spoken of.

True to his promise to Father Kevin, Mark had been attending the Sunday evening services. The first week he had noticed a significant increase in both the number of youth in attendance, and the number of youth participating in the service itself. Ushers, lectors, and even Eucharistic ministers had all been teens. Upon entering the church with Jennifer three weeks ago, they had been greeted by a group of three teens, enthusiastically welcoming them to the liturgy.

One of the teens, on seeing Mark limping, had asked if they would prefer a seat up front. He then escorted them to a spot close to the altar. It was the first time Mark had felt like more than just another face in the crowd. After the service had ended, Mark had been surprised to find that same young man beside him, offering to help him back to his car. Though Mark had turned down the offer, the gesture had left him even more curious as to the changes he had witnessed.

On the way out, Mark had run into Father Kevin and had stopped to greet him. They had talked about Mark's health and how his recovery was going. Though they hadn't been able to talk for long, as Father Kevin had been mobbed by a group of teens who had dragged him off to that evening's youth ministry event.

A similar situation had repeated the following two Sundays. Each week Mark had met a few more teens, and had always made sure to say hello to those he had already met. He had found the vibrant enthusiasm of the young people exhilarating. Their passion had definitely affected the rest of the congregation. Instead of a church filled with hushed conversations and silent prayers before liturgy, the nave had been full of joy, laughter, and hugs.

Smiling at these memories, Mark set down his tea, and then closed his eyes. Perhaps he would find the answers he sought soon. He had a feeling he was getting close. He hoped the homily at Mass that evening would provide more clues. Unfortunately, it didn't. Father Kevin only spoke briefly before introducing a guest speaker to talk about the financial status of the church. However, as the service was about to end, Father Kevin stood and addressed the congregation.

"Since my homily was cut short tonight, I'm going to deliver the rest now," Father Kevin joked, gaining him both laughter and moans. "Seriously, though, I do have one special announcement. Our Youth Ministry program needs volunteers, for both the junior high program, which occurs on Thursday evenings, and high school program, which happens after Mass every Sunday night.

"The dramatic effect we have all experienced these past few months as the teens have accepted greater involvement in the liturgical process with tremendous zeal, is a shining example of what our Catholic faith should be. There is more energy and excitement about being in church than I have ever witnessed before. Our youth program is growing, and growing fast. And, the fervor these teens have for their faith is not only being expressed within these walls. No, they have become true evangelists in their schools and places of employment, every week we see a half-dozen or more new teens being welcomed into the program. Teens from all walks of life, and from a wide range of religious beliefs.

"What we have here before us is an opportunity to participate in their movement. To stand beside our youth and show them that we not only support them in their efforts to grow in their faith, but that we, too, want this revitalization for our own faith. We, too, need a renewal of our spiritual lives."

Father Kevin paused, looking over the sea of faces before him.

"Now, I'm not asking you to decide right now, just to check it out. Brian, the director of the program, will be available after Mass to answer questions. And, he is making tonight's session open for anyone to attend. So, come spend some time this evening with our teens. Check out what is attracting so many young people. See if it might be of interest to you, if it calls to you."

Father Kevin paused again, purposefully turning to face various members of the congregation with a look that said he was speaking directly to them. The last one he connected with was Mark. As their eyes met, Mark felt a warmth spread over him, as if he had just been wrapped in a heavy blanket.

"We are all called to ministry in our own way," Father Kevin continued, his eyes still locked on Mark. "And we all respond in our own way. But what we cannot deny is that we are called, and that we are expected to respond."

Father Kevin held Mark's eyes a bit longer. Mark nodded, giving Father Kevin a look of understanding and agreement. Father Kevin nodded back.

"We simply can't live our lives in denial of our responsibility to discipleship," Father Kevin said, once more addressing the whole congregation, "and then expect that we will be freely welcomed into heaven. Even if we give generously, never sin, and are polite and kind to everyone we meet, we must still do more. Therefore, choose to respond tonight. Don't wait until tomorrow. Don't wait to consider if you're ready or not. Don't wait to make sure God is speaking to you. Trust me, He is speaking to you! If this truly isn't for you, you will have lost nothing more than an hour of your time. Certainly you can give that much for this man who spent three hours dying on a cross for you."

Father Kevin pointed to the crucifix statue on the wall behind the altar as he said those final words. He held his hand raised there for a moment, and then sat back down while one of the choir members began to read the rest of the announcements.

Mark didn't hear a single word, though. There

was a fire burning in his heart. It was as if Father Kevin had been speaking to him alone, as if no one and nothing else mattered. Though he would never have even considered volunteering to help the youth programs on his own, he now could do nothing to resist the urge to respond. He was going to be the first new volunteer that night. Somehow, he knew that doing this would provide the next set of answers he was seeking. The only question he had was if Jennifer would join him.

The final blessing was pronounced and the recessional hymn began. Mark reached for Jennifer's hand, squeezed it once, then paused, squeezed again four times, paused once more, and then squeezed three more times. This had become their silent way of saying 'I love you'. Jennifer shook her hand free and wrapped her arm around his waist.

As he began to sing the closing song, he sang with more enthusiasm and joy than ever done before. He didn't turn and exit the pew after Father Kevin left, but stayed and sang until the choir finished their song. Before stepping into the aisle, Mark looked up at the crucifix behind the altar. A small tear slid down his cheek.

Sunday, November 20

"This is sheer madness," Mark thought as he entered the hall, his eyes wide with surprise, and his mouth agape.

In front of him, a sea of teens were sitting at tables in groups from two or three to as many as a dozen or more. As he watched, box after box of pizza disappeared, as if these youth hadn't eaten in weeks.

Michael Chrobak

Mark searched for Brian, the Youth Minister, finding him in conversation with a group of parents. He carefully wandered over, keeping his hands close to his body. There was no telling how many of his fingers he might lose if he got too close to the feeding frenzy.

Since this was the last youth group of the month, tonight was scheduled as a social night. As Mark had learned in the brief meeting that he and a few other adult volunteers attended with Brian two weeks ago, each week of the month had a different theme.

The first Sunday was always a catechetical night, when the teens learned what the church taught regarding a wide range of social issues, as opposed to what they might have heard in the media or from their friends. The second Sunday of each month focused on social justice, either through guest speaker presentations or with the teens participating in charitable works. The third Sunday was called *Hot Topics*, with discussions focused on recent events of the world. The last meeting of each month, like tonight, was a social night.

Mark had witnessed the first and second Sunday activities already, having volunteered the same night Father Kevin had made his plea. Tonight was Mark's third and final night as an observer. From here, if he chose to return again after the Thanksgiving weekend, he would be an official member of the leadership team.

As Mark neared the group of parents, he overheard them sharing their deep appreciation and support for Brian, as well as thanking him for everything he was doing for their teens. Mark knew that what the parents were really trying to say, was that they were thankful that they, themselves, had found a way to survive their children's teenage years. Brian shrugged off the compliments, not in a vain way, but with pure humility, expressing time and again that the success of the program was not his doing, but God's.

Grabbing a seat against the edge of a table, Mark waited until the parents finished their praise and left the room. Mark wished that even half of them would stay, but they were not allowed. Any parent who had teens in the program could only participate in what was known as 'back office' activities: stuffing envelopes, making copies, gathering supplies or cleaning up.

"Hello, Brian," Mark greeted the Youth Minister.

"Hey there!" Brian responded, a smile stretching across his face. "You wondering where I'm going to put you tonight?"

Mark nodded. The first night he had only been allowed to observe, He had been asked to stay at the back of the room, along with the other new volunteers. A few of the seasoned volunteers were there to answer any questions they might have. On the second night, he had been assigned to shadow one of the adult volunteers during the small group discussion, but as an observer, not a participant.

"Well," Brian began, a mischievous look on his face, "you know how I said last week that this is the week you will participate all the way?"

"Yeah...?" Mark said hesitantly, wondering what he was about to get into.

"That's your job tonight. Participate fully. As if you were one of the teens. Do you feel up to that?"

An anxious feeling shot through Mark's mind as he considered what might be hidden behind Brian's question.

"I'll do my best. I mean, you know I still can't get

around that easy because of this dang blood clot, but I think I can hang with you guys. What are we doing tonight?"

"Oh, you'll see, Mark. You'll see," Brian said, patting Mark on the shoulder as he walked past, bravely entering the throng of teens.

Mark watched as Brian tossed a few high-fives, gave a couple of chest bumps or fist pumps, and shared more than a few hugs as he worked his way deeper into the pack. He could tell the love that Brian had for these kids. And he could see that love and appreciation reflected back. Mark hoped to one day establish the same level of rapport.

Ten minutes later, Mark found out what his commitment to Brian entailed. The teens had been separated into six different groups, a process that could only be described as asking mosquitoes to fly in formation. Difficult though it was, Brian had a few tricks. Eventually, each group held somewhere between fourteen and eighteen teens, two young adult volunteers, and two adults. Mark was in a group with Laura, a fairly diminutive woman in her mid-thirties who made up for her small stature with a commanding voice, giving her the appearance she was much larger than she was. She also appeared to be heavily caffeinated. The amount of energy she had made Mark weary just to watch.

The two young adults that had been filtered into Mark's group were almost as energetic as Laura. The pair of college freshman ladies immediately took charge of the group, ensuring everyone knew each other by name. Mark considered just sitting back and letting the three women run the show, but something inside urged him to let go of any anxiety or concern and to just let things happen as they may.

The first activity planned for the evening was based somewhat on the television show *The Amazing Race*. At various places around the church grounds, stations had been established where the teens would have to complete a challenge before receiving the clue that would lead them to the next station. The only rule was that everyone had to participate in every challenge in some way. To confirm they had completed the challenge, the adults supervising each station would take a group photo, then share it on Twitter using a specific hashtag Brian created for each challenge. The first group who could submit their group photos with the correct hashtags would win the game.

Mark found it all a little confusing, and turned to Laura, hoping she could provide a better explanation. Before he could ask a question, though, an air horn sounded and the race was on. Emily and Sierra, the two young adult leaders, tore open the envelope that contained the first clue. Sierra read the clue out loud.

"A tiny room, this house of gold, holds treasures beyond any foretold," she read, then asked the group, "Anyone have an idea where that might be?"

"House of gold? Like a palace or something?" Tony asked.

"I dunno, maybe," Emily said with a look that said she knew the answer, but couldn't say.

"Or maybe like a shrine or statue," Taylor suggested.

"Statues aren't houses though. If it's holding treasure, it has to be a chest or something," Nick said.

"Where would we find a chest of gold in the church?" asked Patrick.

"What about the Tabernacle? It's gold and it kinda looks like a chest when the doors are open," Tiffany suggested.

"Yes!" screamed Monica. "Let's go!"

The group burst into action, racing as fast as they could towards the main church building. Mark did his best to keep up, pushing himself to walk quickly. By the time he entered the church, his team was already engaged in the challenge. Mark looked over the shoulders of two of the teens as the group huddled around a table. On the top were fourteen pictures, each depicting one of the Stations of the Cross. The challenge for this location was to put the stations in the right order, which the group completed on their third attempt. They posed for their group photo, then received their next clue. This time Emily read the clue.

"Water, water, everywhere, but not a drop to drink. Instead, sit by my flowers, and pause a while to think."

"Okay, this one's weird," Patrick said.

"Maybe it means the baptismal fount where we bless ourselves before church," Taylor suggested.

"Well, I doubt you would drink that water, but there's no flowers there, and no place to sit," Laura reminded the group.

"Oh! I have it!" shouted Nick. "I helped clean up the garden behind the rectory for Boy Scouts a few years ago. There's a large fountain there, and tons of plants with flowers."

"I've been there," Emily said, excitedly. "There's a bench right by the fountain, too. That has to be the place."

Again, the teens raced off to the next station,

leaving Mark hobbling behind once more. He began to wonder if perhaps he had over-estimated his readiness to participate fully as he had promised, but pushed himself to follow along none the less. This time, however, the location was on the other side of the parish grounds, a distance that seemed more daunting with each step. Mark watched his group from a distance as the gap continued to widen. Laura, who was at the back of the group, was busy counting heads.

"We're missing someone," Laura said, getting the group to stop.

The teens looked around, trying to figure out who was missing. Patrick, who was by far the tallest in the group, looked back the way they had just come. Mark waved to him as he hobbled along.

"Got him!" Patrick shouted, and then sprinted out to meet Mark.

Mark anticipated that Patrick would simply help him so he could hobble faster, but, instead, the teen grabbed him around the waist, lifting Mark up in a fireman's carry.

"I got you!" Patrick said as he began jogging back to the group.

"You...sure...I'm...not...too   heavy?" Mark grunted between bounces.

"Nah. We do this at football practice," Patrick said. "By the way, my name's Patrick. But just about everyone calls me Moose."

As he bounced along, Mark began to worry that his lack of mobility would slow the group down, possibly keeping them from finishing in one of the top places. He didn't want to be the reason these teens didn't earn a prize. He also couldn't imagine Patrick carrying him for the rest of the night.

"Thank you, Moose!" Laura said as Patrick carefully placed Mark back on his feet in the midst of the group.

"Maybe I should just drop out and wait for you guys back at the hall?" Mark suggested.

"No way," Patrick replied.

"Moose, you'll wear yourself out before we finish the game!" Laura responded. "We need to find a better way to keep Mark with us. We started as a group, and we'll finish as a group."

"The wheelchair!" Sarah blurted out, then turned and raced back to the church, disappearing for only a moment before triumphantly reappearing, pushing a red and black wheelchair that the church kept on hand in case anyone was in need. She placed the wheelchair behind Mark, holding it steady while he sat down. When he was seated, the group turned back to the challenge. This time, they had to match several pictures of saints to the flower or plant each saint was associated with.

With that challenge complete and the next clue solved, the teens again rushed off in pursuit of the prize, this time with Mark riding in the chair. For the rest of the night this pattern repeated. The group raced from one location to the next, each teen taking a turn pushing Mark in his chair. At some point, the group started making siren sounds as they ran.

The group photos became crazier as well. In one photo, they posed like James Bond. In another, they stood like superheroes. In a third, Laura brought out fake mustaches for everyone to wear. In another, they did a video with everyone frozen like mannequins. It was by far one of the best nights Mark had spent in years. He couldn't remember the last time he had laughed that much.

More than once, the wheelchair almost toppled over as the teen pushing it attempted to take a turn too fast. Mark didn't care, though. He just held on tighter, and laughed. Though physically he was constrained by his injuries, his heart felt free. He was no longer just an observer, no longer an outsider looking in, wondering where, or if, he belonged. He was a part of something exciting.

When the games were over, the teens met back at the church hall for make-your-own sundaes while the awards were handed out. Mark's group had come in fourth place for the challenge, but won the award for Best Group Photos. They also won the award for being the group with the most energy. For that final award, Patrick surprised Mark by picking him up once more in a fireman's hold and carrying him on stage to accept the award.

As the swarm of teens began to migrate out to the parking lot to find their rides home, and the volunteers began to clean up, two of the girls from Mark's group approached him.

"Mr. Counsel? We were wondering something," Ashley said.

"Yeah? What's up, Ashley?" he asked.

"Well, we don't really do closing prayer on game nights. We all just kinda take off," she began.

"But we thought it would be cool if we could pray over you in the Chapel," Briana finished.

Mark sat up straight, a bit overcome by their request. His eyes lit up, and he smiled warmly.

"Yeah? Sure, that would be nice," he said. "But,

please, you can call me Mark."

The two girls smiled, their excitement evident by the gleam in their eyes.

"Okay, Mark!" Briana exclaimed. "We'll go gather the others."

As the two held hands and jogged back to find the rest of the group, Mark paused a moment, considering the effect their request had. He had never been prayed over. He wasn't sure what would be involved. Obviously the teens were comfortable with it, or they wouldn't have asked. Deep in thought, Mark watched as the teens discussed how they wanted to set up for the prayer.

"You really made an impression on your group tonight," Brian said from behind him.

Startled, Mark almost fell as he lurched out of the wheelchair. Brian reached out, catching Mark by the hood of his sweatshirt.

"You okay?" he asked.

"Yeah," Mark replied. "Just didn't hear you standing there. Lost in thought I guess."

"Well, you did really well. Wasn't sure what you were going to do to keep up with your group. I was worried you might give up for a moment."

"What, were you watching me?" Mark asked.

"Yeah, I was," Brian replied. "Tonight was sort of a test, one I make all of my new volunteers pass before they are officially welcomed to the group."

"And? Did I pass?" Mark asked.

"Yeah, you sure did!" Brian smiled. "By the way, you'll notice some of the other new volunteers who joined three weeks ago won't be coming back."

"Can I ask why?"

"Well, the simple story is, they didn't pass the test. Either they decided they weren't cut out for this, or I had to explain it to them."

"Really? You're that strict about volunteers, huh?" Mark asked, a bit shocked that Brian wouldn't just take any help he could get.

"I have to be. These teens are too important to just let anyone hang out. This is a ministry, not some way for adults to reconnect with their lost youth. It takes a special kind of person to work with teens. You can't be too full of yourself, too timid, or too shy. You have to be willing to let the teens see you at your best, and at your worst."

"So, what did I do to make the cut?" Mark asked eagerly.

"First of all, you didn't quit. Even though I could tell you were struggling to keep up, you didn't just walk away. And then, when Moose picked you up, you just let him. You trusted him fully, and you trusted every one of those teens who pushed you in the chair, even when they almost killed you a few times!" Brian explained, pausing a moment before continuing. "But the way you participated in the group photos, it was like you were just one of the kids. You played full out tonight, Mark. I'm really hoping you will keep coming back. These kids need someone like you. You're perfect for this ministry.

"Look, I know your group wants to have a quick prayer for you in the chapel before they leave, and I have to tell you, I don't think I've ever had a group ask to do that for a brand new volunteer. You really touched them. I mean, Moose likes everyone. He's an easy kid to figure out. But the quieter, shy kids you had in your group tonight, I've never seen them participate like they did this evening."

"Well, I'm sure Laura, Emily, and Sierra had a lot to do with that. I was just following along behind them," Mark admitted.

"Actually, those three came to me tonight to tell me they enjoyed having you in their group as well. All three of them gave you a strong recommendation. They want you back as much as I do."

"Wow, Brian. I don't know what to say. I mean, yeah, of course I want to come back. I had a ton of fun tonight."

"Perfect! Then, I look forward to working with you!" Brian exclaimed. "I'll probably pair you up with Laura for another few weeks. You're not quite ready to lead a small group discussion yet. There's still some training we need to do first. But for now, let's get you over to the chapel."

As Mark began to walk towards the door, Brian stopped him.

"Uh-uh, get in," he said, pointing to the wheelchair and giving Mark a huge grin.

Mark replied with a smirk and a shrug, then spun around and sat back in the chair.

"Why not? But you better be the best ambulance-siren-sound-maker of the night!"

Brian got behind the wheelchair. He did a few exercises to prepare, like jumping up and down, stretching his arms, and then yodeling loudly.

"Okay," Brian said. "But, before we go, I just want to say, thanks for choosing the higher ground."

Before Mark could ask him what he meant, they were off and running, with Brian bellowing out siren noises, and Mark holding on tightly.

Monday, November 21

"Hon, we need to talk," Mark said as he took a seat on the couch next to his wife."

Jennifer turned off the television show she was watching, giving her full attention to her husband. This was one of the things Mark appreciated most about his wife. Whenever he said he needed to talk, she never hesitated. Whatever she was doing was put on pause, shut down, or set aside. Mark never felt that he took second place. Unfortunately, he knew he didn't always return the same level of respect. That was one of the many things he was trying to work on.

"What's going on?" she asked.

"You know how I'm supposed to return to work next week, right?" Mark asked.

Jennifer nodded.

"Yeah, I know. I've been thinking about that, too. I mean, I know you're not happy there. I know it stresses you out a lot."

This was another thing Mark appreciated about Jennifer. He had never shared with her how he really felt about his job. The fact that she already knew told him how intuitive she was. It also told him how evident his stress must be, even though he had tried to hide it from her. If it was that evident, then the level of stress he was under was most likely far more than he was admitting to himself.

"Wow," he said. "I didn't realize it was that apparent."

"Are you kidding?" Jennifer said, with a quizzical look. "You come home and hide out for a good

71

half-hour or more before you even say 'hello' to me. You head out to the yard and start watering a section of lawn that doesn't need to be watered. Or you clean and organize the workbench in the garage, even though it looks like it was last cleaned by someone with a major case of OCD. Yeah, I would say your stress is pretty apparent."

Mark considered her words carefully. He knew what she said was true. He would come home, change his clothes, and then disappear. Sometimes there really were chores that needed to be done. But most often he spent that time reviewing again and again the events of his day. He would replay every conversation, reconsider every decision he had made, and reexamine each new relationship he had established. All that stress just to move up one more rung on the corporate ladder. And for what reason? So that he could have even more pressure and stress?

Even after Mark spent that time alone, trying to separate himself from the demands of his job, his mind never stopped. Over and over again he would replay the memories of the day, creating a different ending each time. This left Mark berating himself for not having chosen one of those potential alternate options. Silently, his mind continued to challenge his ability, looking for one more reason to make him believe he was failing at his job.

It wasn't just work-related items that his mind would chastise him about. His relationship with his wife; whether or not he had been a good father; his weight; even his recent financial decisions. Nothing was safe. This voice rarely had anything positive to say. Because of this, Mark rarely gave himself any praise. This was why he had a difficult time accepting praise from anyone else, too. In many ways, Mark was convinced he wasn't worthy.

But last night, as he had sat inside the circle of teens, their hands on his back, shoulders, and head, Mark heard something he never had before. His inner voice was silent. It was as if the words of their prayers released a hidden, secret strength he never knew. He felt far more powerful, capable and appreciated than he had ever felt before. For the first time in as long as Mark could remember, he had felt as if he belonged.

"If it's that apparent to you that I've been stressed," Mark asked Jennifer, "then why didn't you ever say anything?"

"I don't know," she replied. "I suppose part of me didn't think it was my place to say something. I figured it was something you needed to sort out for yourself. Besides," Jennifer admitted, "whenever I did try, I don't think you even heard a word I was saying. It was as if you were so lost in your own thoughts that nothing else registered."

"I don't want to go back to that. I can't go back to that," Mark admitted to his wife.

"Then don't," Jennifer responded, surprising Mark. "Sure, you make good money, but it's not worth trading your happiness, or your health, for something that is temporary."

Jennifer reached out and held Mark's hand.

"Look, we don't need a lot of the stuff we have. We don't need to spend as much money as we do every month. We can seriously learn to cut back. Not just a little, but a lot. And I think we'll find that when we do, we won't miss what we give up. I don't like how it feels as if we're always chasing after something we can't catch, and I don't think you do either. I've taken a look at our finances and I think we can get by without you working. It will be a stretch, at least at first, but I'm comfortable that we can do it."

"Really? I don't know, Jen. I mean, I've been working at one job or another since I was a teen. Before that even, if you count my paper route. Honestly? I don't know what I would do with myself if I wasn't going into work every day."

"Well, maybe it's time to find out," Jennifer said, squeezing his hand.

She stood up, letting go of his hand.

"I'm going to make a cup of tea, do you want one?" she asked him.

"Sure," Mark said, his mind racing once more with imaginations of what his future might look like.

This time, however, when his inner voice hit him with negativity, he simply shut it out. He wasn't interested in hearing negativity any longer. It was time for a change, and it would have to start from within.

Chapter Five
Admission

But if we walk in the light, as he is in the light,
we have fellowship with one another - 1 John 1:7

Thursday, November 24

"Mark!" Jennifer called out. "Let everyone know we're ready to eat, okay?"

"You got it, babe," he replied, reaching for the television remote.

"I'll check out back," his son Robert said as Mark shut off the television.

"I got the garage," his daughter Kathy offered, following her brother out of the room.

Mark stood up, about to head towards the front door.

"Don't worry, Dad. I'll check out front. You go sit down," his youngest daughter, Autumn, told him as she hurdled the baby gate that blocked the hallway leading to the front of the house.

"Well, that pretty much takes care of it," Mark said to a suddenly empty room.

He gathered the few drinks that were spread throughout the room and took them to the dining room table. He placed the glasses where he knew each of his children would sit. It had been years since his kids had lived under his roof, but they still migrated to their familiar place at the table whenever they came home. In these moments, they would fall back to the behaviors of their childhood. Even the way they joked with and teased each other made it feel as if the years since they had moved out had never passed.

Before taking his usual chair at the head of the table, Mark went back to the kitchen to ensure there was nothing his wife and daughter-in-law needed help with. As expected, they chased him out quickly, letting him know they had it under control. Mark stayed just a moment anyway, the sight and smell of the Thanksgiving feast holding him captive.

"Don't you dare touch anything," Jennifer teased as Mark went to get a closer look at the turkey.

"I won't," he replied. "I promise."

"Oh, go ahead, dad," his daughter-in-law, Evelyn, said as she held out a basket of fresh biscuits.

"Just a small one, perhaps," Mark said, grinning mischievously.

"You're just bad. You know that?" Jennifer scolded him jokingly.

Mark tore a small piece of biscuit and held it out for Jennifer to take. She raised her hands as if to guard herself from him, turning her head to the side as she did. When Mark looked away, thinking she didn't want it, she leaned forward suddenly, grabbing the biscuit, and part of Mark's finger, in her teeth.

Mark jumped back in shock, dropping the rest of his biscuit as he wrapped his fingers in his other hand. He looked at his wife, his eyes wide with surprise. Jennifer looked back, her eyes shimmering with playfulness, a sly smile on her face. Mark held his hand out in front of him, making an overly dramatic show of counting his fingers. Jennifer giggled.

"Oh, don't be a baby. I didn't really bite you," she said.

Mark smiled, then leaned forward and gave her a quick kiss. As she was about to pull away, he kissed her once more, this time with passion. When he finally let her go, she remained frozen for a moment. Her eyes were still closed, and she had a warm glow on her cheeks. Slowly, her mouth stretched into a loving smile. She opened her eyes and looked at her husband with a tenderness he hadn't seen for some time. Not because it wasn't there, but because he hadn't taken the time to look. They stood there, wrapped in the moment, the world around them fading away.

"Um...hate to break the moment," Evelyn said meekly, "but I gotta get something off the stove."

Jennifer blushed as she realized they hadn't been alone, and then stepped back to allow Evelyn to pass, Mark gave his wife a wink, and then nodded his head towards the biscuit on the floor.

"You made me drop my biscuit," he said, reaching for another one from the basket.

"Go," Jennifer said, pointing to the passageway out of the kitchen. "Or I'll bite you again!"

"I'm going, I'm going! Let me just pick this up," Mark said, reaching down to retrieve the biscuit off the floor, not taking his eyes off Jennifer's face.

Without looking, he tossed the biscuit in the sink, then slowly backed out of the kitchen. With his eyes still locked on his wife, he inched his way into the hallway, his body slowly disappearing around the bend. With his head the only part remaining, and his eyes still locked on his wife, he whispered, 'I love you'. Jennifer whispered back, 'I love you, too'.

"Aww," Evelyn sighed. "That's so cute."

Back in the dining room, Mark reached into his shirt pocket and pulled out an index card. On the face of the card was a list he had created earlier that morning. The list contained all of the things he wanted to remember to be thankful for. He read the list over once more, making sure there was nothing else he might want to add. Convinced the list was complete, he placed it back in his pocket and sat down.

The noise level inside the house increased significantly as his grandchildren flooded in. Of the five grandchildren, the oldest was twelve and the youngest, three. One by one they took their seats at a small table nearby while the adults filled in the chairs at the main table. When everyone was gathered, Mark looked around the room.

On each side sat his two older children. Kathy was on his left, and Robert sat on his right. Nicholas, Kathy's husband, sat next to Kathy, with Autumn on Nick's left. Evelyn sat next to her husband, Robert. The chair to her right was empty. Jennifer sat directly across from him.

Conversation among the adults continued to jump from one topic to another as everyone got settled. Mark remained silent, watching the scenario around him unfold. He thought back to his hospital stay, just less than two months ago. He realized how close he had come to missing out on this holiday, and every holiday after that, too. The fact that he was here in this room experiencing the laughter and joy with his family was by far what he was most grateful for.

Mark watched as Robert filled the wine glasses. Glancing to his right, he watched as Robert's son, Stuart, did the same at the kid table (with sparkling cider instead of wine, of course). Stuart was Robert's oldest child, and was a spitting image of Robert when he was that age. His physical appearance, personality, and mannerisms were carbon copies of what Mark remembered from Robert's childhood. When all the glasses were filled, Mark stood up to address the room.

"I've been thinking a lot today about what I'm grateful for. In fact, I even took the time to write a list so that I wouldn't forget," Mark said as he pulled the index card out of his pocket. "But as I stand here in the midst of this family, everyone here that I love so much, I wonder if the words I wrote down will be enough to express exactly what I feel in my heart."

Mark paused a moment, his throat suddenly tight. Glancing at his wife, he saw a glimmer in her eyes. As their eyes locked together, he could tell she was just as grateful that he was there as well.

"I love you all so much. More than I realized I did before the hospital. Coming that close to death really makes a person reevaluate their priorities and take stock of what's most important. And I couldn't think of anything more important to me than the group of faces looking back at me now."

Mark heard sounds of sniffling as those around the table began to quietly cry. It was more than he could handle. As his eyes, too, began to fill with tears, he turned his head to face towards the table where his grandchildren sat. He could see that his words had affected the older kids as well, which caused Mark to sob even more.

"Is Papa crying?" Stephanie, the youngest grandchild, whispered to Aubrey, her older cousin.

"Yes, he is," Aubrey replied, picking her younger cousin up and nestling her against her chest.

For at least a minute, no one said a word. The only sound was that of his family trying to fight back tears. Eventually, Mark found his composure.

"I'm sorry about that," Mark said, laughing awkwardly as he wiped at the wetness staining his face. "I'm a little more emotional than I thought I would be. Honestly, I don't know if I can manage reading through this list."

"I'll read it for you, Grandpa," one of the grandchildren said.

Mark looked over to see Trevor walking over to the main table, holding out his hand to take the card from Mark. When he was close enough, Mark lifted the six-year-old up, and held him close for a moment.

"It's okay Trev," he said. "Grandpa got this. But you can help me out, okay?"

"How, Papa?" Trevor replied.

"By making me as strong as you are."

"Like this, Papa?" he asked, lifting his arms up high, and flexing his muscles while his face twisted into a grimace.

"Exactly like that, Trevor. That's perfect," he said as he put his grandson back down. "You go back to your seat, but keep making Papa strong, okay?"

Trevor growled, flexing his arms once more, then walked back to his chair.

"I can do that too, Papa! Watch this!" Stephanie said, making the meanest face she could, and growling until her face turned red.

"That's perfect, pumpkin. Thank you," Mark said, turning his attention to the adult table.

"In fact, why doesn't everyone help Papa out, huh? Let's see who can make the best strongman face!" he said.

Mark watched as his entire family began to flex their arms, scrunch up their faces, and growl as best as they could. He began to smile, which grew into a chuckle, and quickly turned to laughter. The laughter spread like wildfire around the room. As it died out, Mark once more looked at his family, his smile refusing to fade.

"I think Papa is as strong as he's ever going to get," he said. "So, let me continue, and I promise this will be brief...and hopefully without any more tears."

He waited as his family settled back into their chairs, and then began once more.

"Of course, I'm extremely thankful for being able to share this day, and hopefully many, many more. And I know I wouldn't be here if it not for the care I received, so let's all take a moment to remember the doctors and nurses who did such a great job of helping bring me back to health.

"But, you know, it's easy to be thankful for all of the good people in our lives. It's easy to be thankful for the people who are there to help us, the ones who love us and take care of us. It's easy to be grateful when you know that your gratitude is going to be accepted and returned. But I wonder about all those who we don't think of when we express gratitude. What about the people who we don't feel like appreciating? Don't they deserve our gratitude as well? Think about it. If everyone we met always treated us with respect, wouldn't we just come to expect it? And, if we expect it, then would we really appreciate and be grateful for it? I don't think so.

"And so, today, I want to share my gratitude for anyone in my past who I believed did something to hurt me, took advantage of me, or caused me pain. Because, without them, I doubt I would ever have learned to appreciate the people I do really care about."

Mark paused, looking around the table. There was only one thing left he wanted to share. Something he would need an extra dose of courage before saying out loud. Reaching for his glass, he took a drink, letting the warmth of the wine coax the words out from within.

"I also don't think that I would have ever reached the decision I made just a few days ago. I haven't told you all yet, because I wanted to wait until we were all together, but I quit my job."

Around the table, shocked gasps filled the air.

"I know, I know, you're all probably surprised at that. But, over the last couple of weeks I've been recovering, I've been thinking a lot about what I value most in my life. I've looked at what I no longer want to be a part of, and I've started to take action to replace the stressful parts of my life with things I really do care about."

"Wow, Dad," Robert interrupted, "So what are you going to do next?"

"Believe it or not, your dad is now a youth ministry volunteer at the church!" Mark responded, pausing to see their reaction. The silent stares lingered longer than he had hoped they would.

"That's great, Dad," Autumn said, breaking the silence. "How long have you been doing that?"

"I've been helping out for a few weeks now," Mark shared, "and I have to tell you, I've never had so much fun. The kids are great, really great. It's by far one of my favorite new activities. I'm learning so much about the church, about our faith."

"I really think that's great," Autumn repeated, giving her father a warm, loving smile. "I know we are all happy for you."

"Thanks, Autumn. Of course, that's not all. I mean, that's just one day a week. For the rest of the time, well, I'm going to take that time to heal. And I mean really heal. Not just my body, but emotionally and spiritually too. Maybe I'll travel a bit, come spend some time with each of you, if you'll have me. Maybe I'll learn to play an instrument, take up painting, or write a book. I want to take this time to find what I really love to do.

"Honestly, this is the happiest I have ever been with any decision I have ever made. The peace I feel inside as I think about all of the opportunities that are in front of me is, quite simply, awesome. I can now do more to give back, to be a person of value, and to help others. I am so looking forward to what my future holds, now more than any other time in my life."

Mark put the index card back in his shirt pocket, realizing that he hadn't even read through the list he had created. Yet, in some way, what actually happened felt so much better.

"Dad," Robert said softly, "I'm proud of you. You've always worked so hard to make sure we all had everything we need. It's about time you started to get everything you need, too."

"I agree, one-hundred percent," Evelyn shared, raising her wine glass.

Mark looked at Kathy, wondering what was going on in her mind. The face that looked back at him was filled with respect and love. Rather than express her thoughts in words, she stood up and came over to her father, wrapping her arms around him tightly.

"I love you so much, Dad," she said. "You have always been my greatest inspiration."

"I love you too, sweetheart. More than you'll ever know," Mark said, returning the hug.

They held each other for a few seconds more, then let go. Kathy returned to her chair, wiping tears from her eyes.

"Now that that's all done, who's ready to eat?" Mark said.

A chorus of 'me, me, me!' echoed from the kid's table.

"Alright, then, whose turn is it to pray?"

Robert raised his arm.

"I believe it's mine, Dad," he said.

"Well, then," Mark began, "who remembers how we begin?"

"That's easy, Papa," Stephanie said raising her hand to her forehead. "In the name of the Father..."

The rest of the room joined in, "...and of the Son..."

Saturday, November 26

"You okay up there, Dad?" Autumn called out as she peered into the darkness at the top of the attic ladder, waiting for her father to reappear from the shadows.

"Yeah," Mark responded. "I dropped the tree stand. Nothing broke. Just a lot of noise."

"I still don't think you should be up there. Not

with your leg still healing and all."

"I've done this every year since you were five," Mark said, trying to sound confident.

Truth was, he was having more difficulty retrieving the Christmas decorations from the storage space in the attic than he had in previous years. Although he had reached a point where he could put full weight on his leg, he still hadn't returned to full strength. His stamina was ebbing rapidly, and more than half of the boxes still needed to be retrieved.

Reaching back down, he picked the tree-stand off the ground, then precariously picked his way back to the ladder leading down into the garage. He had to step only on the rafters, as there was no true floor in the makeshift attic space.

"Someday," he thought, *"I'll get rid of all the useless crap we are storing down below. Then most of this stuff won't need to be stored up here."*

Mark and his wife were by no means hoarders, and they had cleaned out this same garage at least three other times in the fifteen years they had lived here. But stuff had a tendency to accumulate. Most often, the items they got rid of during one of their every-four-years cleanings, were items they had, at the time, considered too valuable to let go. It wasn't until years later that they realized the items they had such trouble getting rid of were still in the exact same spot they had stored them. Meaning, they had never been used. It had been just over three years since the last cleaning. The garage was well overdue.

Mark handed the tree stand down to Autumn, then turned carefully, never letting go of at least one handhold as he stepped back to the stack of Christmas still waiting to be brought down. He thought back to the many times that he had performed this task over the years. At first, the kids had been too young to help, so he had to handle the task on his own. A few years later, Robert had offered to help out, and then, when Robert left for college, Autumn took over.

The two had established a routine that they would not deviate from. The lights went up the Saturday after Thanksgiving. Each year, the first item crossed off the list was a trip to Starbucks for peppermint mochas. They wouldn't take a sip until they were back at home, had turned on the speaker in the garage, and were blasting Christmas carols.

Then the process of retrieving the decorations began. The storage bins came down first. These were stacked in four piles, according to which location of the house or yard they would be used. One pile for items that would be used on the exterior of the house, one for the yard, another that would be used to decorate one of their two Christmas trees. The final pile held the items Jennifer would use to decorate the inside of the house.

Jennifer absolutely loved Christmas. It was by far her favorite time of the year. Every available moment she had from Thanksgiving until Christmas was spent dressing up the inside of the house and their two trees. Most years, she would find at least a dozen or more items to add to her ever-growing collection. Just last year she had announced it was time to find a spot for a third tree.

Mark hoped that wouldn't be this year, though. All of this stuff he was straining to get down would eventually have to go back up. Typically, that happened the weekend after New Year's Day, when all of the kids had returned back to their lives, leaving Mark in charge of managing the cleanup alone.

Finally, about an hour after they brought the first of the bins down, the final bin was retrieved and the attic ladder folded away. Now it was time for the next phase of their plan - another Starbucks run. This time, Mark opted for an eggnog latte, Autumn chose caramel brulee, and they both ordered their drinks with an extra shot of espresso.

Back at home, with the music once more blasting, the overly-caffeinated pair began to hang the lights. Each string was plugged in and tested to ensure that they were in working order before being placed on the house. Being well organized was something Mark took pride in. After the first year that they had lived in this house, he had taken the time to label each spool of lights as they came back down in January. This way, all he had to do each year was to find 'Spool #1', and start hanging.

"Hand me the next set of lights," Mark called out from the top of a ladder.

"Here you go. I checked them already. They're good," Autumn replied.

Mark began twisting the ends of the string he had just installed with the one Autumn handed him. This would ensure they wouldn't come apart on a windy day. Confident they were secure, he began to hang the lights along the gutter, as Autumn held the ladder for him.

"So, Dad, I've been thinking," Autumn said when there was a break in the music playing in the garage.

"Yeah? About what?" he inquired.

"About what drove you to quit your job, and what you think you might be getting into next," she replied as Mark climbed down to reposition the ladder.

"I mean, I know you said you were going to take some time off, but I just don't see you doing that. Remember when you hurt your back a few years ago and were off work for a month?"

"Yeah, I remember. How could I forget? I couldn't walk for three weeks! And it took me more than a year before I could run again. What about it?"

"Well, you might not remember, but I do. You were really antsy that whole time. Like, you couldn't even sit still. You must have re-organized the kitchen cabinets five times once you were able to stand again."

Mark laughed to himself. She was right. He wasn't the type of person who could do nothing. Even taking a vacation was hard for him, unless they planned out two or three activities for each day.

"I know, I know. But this time is different," he explained.

"How so?" she asked, curious how her father might be changing.

"Well, for one, I've never almost died before," he began. "That's something that will really stop you in your tracks, make you think about every part of your life. And, to be honest, most of my activity back then was just that...activity. It didn't matter if it had any purpose or not, I just had to keep moving.

"The thing is, I wasn't really going anywhere. It was more that I was just making sure I didn't stop. I guess, in a way, if I had stopped, then I might have had time to reflect on where my life was. And, to be honest, I've been afraid of facing that reality for a long time now."

Mark paused to watch his daughter, looking for how his words might be affecting her emotionally. He knew she looked up to him, that she had once told him he was her rock. For her to see this more vulnerable side of him was something new, and very different from the father she typically got to see. Yet, he also knew that lying to her, or hiding the truth in any way, would be just another way of preventing himself from facing the truth. It would not be choosing the higher ground.

"I don't get what you mean. What about your life have you been afraid of?" Autumn asked, a puzzled expression on her face.

Mark paused a moment, searching for the right words to say, not wanting to give his daughter any concern about his current emotional or psychological state of mind.

"Autumn, your dad wasn't the super-strong guy you might have thought I was when you were growing up. In fact, I've spent most of my life being afraid. Afraid I wasn't good enough, afraid I would never really make it, afraid of being hurt. Over the years, I got really good at hiding my fear, making others believe that I was a confident, outgoing person. When, in reality, deep inside my own mind I was certain that they would one day find out who and what I really was.

"But, don't worry. That's all in the past now. I've come to terms with my fears, and I've forgiven myself for all the times that I didn't do the right thing, didn't take a chance, or do what *I* wanted to do. All that action just for the sake of action isn't who I am going to be any longer. In fact, it really doesn't matter what I wind up doing going forward. As long as I'm not doing it to hide, to keep other people from seeing how afraid I am, then that's what I'll do."

Autumn reached out and held her dad's hand.

She had a slight glimmer in her eye, and a look of compassion on her face.

"Oh, Dad. There's something you need to understand. For the past few years, I've known about your fears. Not what they were based on, but I could tell you were scared. That's why I've been telling you how much I admire your strength. To me, a strong person isn't someone who can do anything with no fear. It's the person who knows their fear is real, and yet, they move forward anyway. That's what makes people strong. That's what makes you so strong, too.

"Anyone can step up and take a risk if they have no fear of failure, or fear of being hurt. But the people who push themselves beyond their own limitations, who have to push themselves past their own fears, they are the real heroes in this world."

Autumn paused, took a deep breath, and placed the back of her hand against her mouth as she fought back tears.

"That's why you've been my hero since junior high, Dad. That's why I've told you I want to be just like you someday. Because, I'm afraid too. I've been afraid since grade school. And I don't want to be anymore."

Mark was taken back by her words. This was supposed to be his tough kid, the one that stood up for what she believed in, who protected others, especially those most vulnerable. At school, she had made the leadership team, the soccer team, the diving team, and almost made the boys baseball team. This was the kid who had broken her wrist during a soccer match, and had stayed in at goalie. Mark had always thought that she had been born with her mother's strength and character. To find out that she was just as good at hiding her fears as he was opened a new door in their relationship. Mark had a feeling this new door would lead them both to someplace wonderful.

He reached out his arms, hugging his daughter as close to his chest as he could. Autumn buried her face in his shirt, and together they cried for the freedom found by letting go of their false bravado. Neither of them knew the importance of this moment, but they still couldn't disregard the experience they just shared.

"Come on," Mark said eventually, as the two ran out of tears. "Let's get this house decorated. Then we can go share a beer out back and talk some more."

"Yeah," Autumn sighed. "That sounds good."

As Mark let go of his daughter and turned back to climb the ladder once more, he paused and gave her a loving look.

"I love you, kiddo," he said.

"I love you more," she replied.

Mark knew the next thing she expected him to say would be 'I love you most'. They had played this game since she was old enough to talk. Instead, something inside made him change his words.

"You know, I think you just might," he said, reaching out to rub the top of her head.

Chapter Six
Reflection

*By this all people will know that you are my disciples,
if you have love for one another - John 13:15*

Sunday, December 18

Mark leaned against the small desk set at the front of the room. His left leg was crossed over his right, keeping the weight off the slowly recovering limb. His head was bent forward, his eyes focused on the papers he held in his hand. The classroom was silent and still. This was the sixth time that he had read through his notes. That wasn't his normal practice. The other nights he had led a group, he had given the Leader's Guide no more than a perfunctory review. But tonight was different.

Tonight he would be leading a small group on his own. This would be the first time he would not have another adult leader in the room with him. There would be no one to turn to for answers, no one to provide support if the conversation lagged. It was no wonder his nerves were flaring.

Outside the open door of his room, Mark could hear the chaos that was youth ministry as the teens began to migrate from the church hall towards the classrooms. He had, at most, another minute left to prepare. Mark turned and looked behind him, making sure a Bible and a copy of the Catechism of the Catholic

Church were well within reach. Since he was still very much in a learning process himself, he had no qualms about using the resources provided. The last thing he wanted to do was pretend that he knew the answer to a question.

This wasn't like his job, his previous job in sales that is, where he had spent most of his career. During those years, if a customer asked a question he didn't know the answer to, it wasn't beyond him to make something up just to close the sale. But that wouldn't work with teens. First of all, they were smarter than that. He knew they could read when someone was bluffing, and far more accurately than his customers had. Second, he couldn't risk one of the teens going home and telling their parents what they learned at church, especially if what he taught wasn't correct.

And so he had studied and reviewed, and studied some more. It wasn't that the topic for the night had appeared difficult. They weren't going to be talking about drugs and alcohol, or premarital sex. Those would be difficult conversations to have even for a veteran volunteer. Tonight the topic was on charity. At first, he had been enthused when he saw the topic for this night. He believed that he and his wife had always been charitable people. Jennifer was involved in volunteer work with a social advocacy group, and Mark had participated in planning and coordinating the annual food drive at his company. Yet, the further he dove into the topic, the more he realized that what he thought were charitable acts, sometimes weren't that at all.

Movement at the doorway brought him back to the present moment. As the teens began to file in, Mark studied their faces. He had learned how to pick out which kids would be the most active participants and which ones would need the most encouragement, simply by the way they entered the room. It wasn't always the loudest, most active teens that chose to share, either. Sometimes it was those who appeared to be quiet that had the most to say.

The last few teens entered the room, taking a seat on the floor in an almost perfect circle. Mark took a seat on the top of the desk, letting his legs dangle freely. He waited while the conversation in the room slowly drifted to silence, and then addressed his group.

"Good evening! Most of you I have already met, but I see a few new faces in here as well. So, we're going to start tonight with a quick round of introductions. Nothing fancy, just your name, where your family will be spending Christmas, and what animal you would want as a pet, if you could have it. And, just to get your minds into the process of creative thinking, none of the typical pets this round. No dogs, cats, birds, fish or rodents of any type."

"Does that include guinea pigs? Are those rodents?" one of the teens asked.

Mark smiled as he pointed to the speaker, drawing a look of surprise from the young man..

"First rule in my room, if you speak out of turn, you get to go first!" Mark announced, adjusting to a more comfortable position.

"What, me?" the young man asked, with a puzzled look.

"Yes, you! Since you're so eager to share. Go ahead and begin, then pick who goes next," Mark said, tossing a small, red bean bag to him.

"What do I share again?" the boy asked his

neighbor.

"Oh, man, Tony. Really? Don't you ever pay attention? Your name, where you're gonna spend Christmas, and what pet you want," the girl replied.

"Oh yeah, I got it. Well, as Taylor already said, my name is Tony. My family is going to my grandma's for Christmas. She lives down by Disneyland, so we might spend a day there," he said, tossing the bean bag to another teen across the room.

"You forgot your pet," Mark informed him.

"Ha! Yeah, I did. Well, I don't know. Maybe a monkey. Or a llama. Something like that."

"Monkeys and llamas aren't even related!" another teen blurted out.

"Well now, that bring us to rule number two. No insults or talking down to anyone. Whenever someone shares, we accept their point of view without judgment. It might not match our view, but that doesn't make it wrong. Maybe in Tony's mind there is something that relates monkeys and llamas," Mark stated.

"Yeah, they both stink!" Tony stated, scrunching his face and holding his nose.

The room broke into laughter for a moment, Mark joining in along with the teens..

"Okay, okay, settle down, or it's going to take all night to just get through introductions. Let's keep it going. Who has the beanbag?" Mark asked, raising his voice just slightly.

"I do," said a female voice as she held the beanbag up for everyone to see. "I'm Sarah. My family isn't going anywhere this year, we're staying at home."

"Lame," one of the boys whispered, perhaps not realizing the whole room could hear him.

"Okay, hold on, that was a violation of rule number two," Mark said, turning to face the boy who just spoke. "What's your name?"

"Robert," the boy responded, a look of concern on his face.

"Robert, this is what I was just talking about. Sometimes we say things that we think might be funny, but really aren't. I'm guessing that you have no idea why Sarah's family isn't traveling this year."

Robert turned his face, looking away. Mark could see that the teen was regretful for the interruption. Turning his gaze to the left, Mark measured the expression on Sarah's face, trying to determine if he should encourage her to share. Unable to ascertain her emotional state, he took the risk.

"Sarah? Do you feel like sharing with the room why you're not going anywhere this year? It's okay if you say you don't want to."

Sarah sat crossed legged, her head facing the floor, absentmindedly picking at some of the trim on the side of her shoe. Her hair flowed forward, preventing Mark from seeing her face.

"Yeah, I guess," she said slowly. "It's 'cause of my dad. He's got cancer. They aren't sure how much longer he's going to be alive. We don't go any-where these days. Except to the hospital for one of his treatments."

Mark let her words sink in, and then turned to face Robert.

"You see, sometimes what's funny in our minds can be hurtful to someone else. Even though we don't mean it to be. We think we're telling a joke, or that we're just teasing, but our words can cause others pain. And since this kind of pain is only felt on the inside, we don't always see it. In fact, we may never know," Mark stated empathetically.

Robert wouldn't look at him. He remained focused on some random object at the back of the room. Mark could see he was regretting his choice of words, though. There was remorse in the boy's eyes.

"We'll talk more about this later tonight. In fact, our topic on charity couldn't have been planned on a better night," Mark said, pausing once more as he watched Sarah for a moment. "Sarah? Do you want to continue? I think you still need to tell us your pet, and then pass the bag to someone else, okay?"

"Right now I don't want any pets," Sarah said as she tossed the bag across the room. "They just die too."

The final words held the room captive. Mark searched for the right words to say. While he waited for his mind to find them, an inner voice whispered, *"Sit down, on the floor. Be vulnerable."* And so he did.

As he settled into his new position, a warm sensation grew inside his heart, spreading rapidly, until his whole body tickled with warmth. Even the pain he almost always felt in his leg was gone. As if on cue, his mouth began to move and words formed of their own accord.

"Sarah, I want you to know that I feel your pain right now. What you are going through, the weight of the burden you have been asked to carry. I understand. There have been times when I felt like my world was falling apart, too. But I want you to know one thing, and I want you to believe me when I tell you this. You will get through this. Yes, it will be tough, maybe tougher than anything you've had to face before, but you won't lose everything. Hold on to what is good. I know that might seem impossible right now, but you have to have hope. Hope is something that no one can take from you."

Mark paused a moment, giving Sarah a chance to fight back the tears that had formed while he spoke. He reached his hand behind him, retrieving a box of tissue from the corner of the desk, and gave it to the teen sitting on his left. Mark watched as the box made its way around the room. Sarah wasn't the only one in need of Kleenex right now. Most of the other girls, and a few of the boys, had joined in her sorrow. The emotions filled the room like heavy smoke, making it hard for Mark to see, his throat tightened as he swallowed.

"Do you want to stay with the group? Or would you rather head over to the chapel?"

As part of his training, Mark had been told to offer time in the chapel to any teen who had become emotional, troubled by the conversations, or simply needed a break from sharing. Two adult volunteers trained in child psychology and counseling were always stationed inside, just in case they were needed. The last thing Brian wanted was for a teen to carry a painful experience home with them.

Sarah shook her head, keeping her eyes locked on the floor.

"I'm okay," she whispered. "We can move on."

"If anything changes, or you need a break, just let me know, okay?"

She nodded again, lifting her face just enough to glance in his direction.

"Okay, then. For those who haven't introduced themselves yet, let's just go around from my left, and just say your first name, nothing else. We'll get to know more about each other later."

The teens took turns in order, following Mark's instruction. When the last teen on his right had taken his turn, Mark reached for the Bible.

"Robert," he said, holding the book out in front of him, "I'd like for you to read tonight."

Robert turned to face him. Mark could tell by the way Robert looked at him that the boy had expected a harsher punishment than just reading out loud. Perhaps at an earlier time in his life, Mark would have scolded the boy in front of the group, sent him to the Youth Minister's office, or had his parents come pick him up. Tonight, he didn't feel like doing any of those. Tonight he only had compassion for the young man whose actions, Mark understood, had not been done with malicious intent.

"I also need a volunteer to lead prayer. Who hasn't done that in a while?"

No hands went up. Mark had expected that. Getting teens to read out loud was one thing. Getting them to pray out loud was a completely different struggle.

"I can do it," Alyssa said, raising her hand. "Can I get a piece of paper and a pencil first?"

"Of course. You know where they are. And thank you, Alyssa," Mark said.

Alyssa half crawled, half duck-walked to the supply bin and grabbed the items she needed, and then shuffled back to her place. After a moment's thought, she began scribbling words on the page.

"The first scripture today comes from the Old Testament, from Deuteronomy. And the second, from the New Testament, from the book of Hebrews," Mark informed the group, then turned to check on Alyssa. "Are you almost ready?"

She nodded silently, keeping her focus on her work.

"Okay, go ahead Robert," Mark said, nodding in the boy's direction.

Robert sat up and cleared his throat.

"If there is among you anyone in need, a member of your community in any of your towns within the land that the Lord your God is giving you, do not be hard-hearted or tight-fisted towards your needy neighbors. You should rather open your hand, willingly lending enough to meet the need, whatever it may be," he read aloud, pausing just a moment before flipping the pages to the next bookmark.

"Let mutual love continue," he read with a gentle yet persuasive voice. "Do not neglect to show hospitality to strangers, for by doing that some have entertained angels without knowing it. Remember those who are in prison, as though you were in prison with them; those who are being tortured, as though you yourselves were being tortured."

Robert closed the Bible and handed it to the teen sitting next to him, who in turn passed it to the next one in line. As Mark waited for the book to make its way back to him, he kept his eyes focused on Robert, waiting to catch his attention. When the young man looked his way, Mark gave him a smile and a nod to show his appreciation for the reverence in which he had completed his task. Robert blushed slightly as he smiled back. Mark felt a gentle tap on his leg as the Bible was placed in his lap. Nodding once more to Robert, Mark turned his attention to the entire group.

"Let's begin as we always do, in the name of the Father..." he said, slowly starting the sign of the cross, allowing the teens to follow along.

When they finished the opening blessing, he then gave a nod to Alyssa, letting her know that she could begin. Alyssa laid her notes out in front of her, and then bowed her head. Mark could see her take a deep breath, allowing the silence in the room to draw everyone's attention to what she was about to say. Mark could sense that there was a deeper spirituality within the young people in his group, a reverence that he, too, had felt at their age, but had been too timid to express.

"God, we ask that you are present with us tonight as we talk about charity," Alyssa began. "We ask that you let us all be honest and patient with our words, showing our friends and even those we haven't met yet the respect that they deserve. Let us remember that we are all carrying different burdens, that we all have things in our lives that make us sad, especially during the holidays.

"Help us to remember those who don't have what we have, and to not be jealous of those who have more. Remind us of the reason for this holiday. That it's not about gifts and getting, it's about love and giving. Thank you for coming into the world to help us understand this. Amen."

The rest of the room echoed her 'Amen', blessing themselves once more. Mark took a quick look at his notes, and then addressed the room.

"Okay, so before we start with our discussion, I'm going to give you five minutes to come up with what you think is the best definition for the word 'charity'," he said.

He reached into the supply bin behind him, taking out enough slips of paper and pencils for the group. He divided them into two equal piles, passing half the items to his left and half to his right, waiting until they reached the back of the group.

"Take your time, and use your own words. Don't put your name on the paper, just your definition. Then fold the paper and pass them back up here so that I can read them to the group. Tell me what *you* think charity means," he instructed, watching as the teens turned their attention to the task.

While he waited, Mark thought once more about what charity meant to him. He recognized that in the past it had just been one more action he took. Nothing more than activity for the sake of activity. He would complete the task, whether it was donating old clothing to St. Vincent de Paul, collecting food for the poor, or giving a homeless person the loose change in his pocket, and then he would just go back to doing something else. The positive feelings generated during the act never lasted more than a moment or two, and Mark saw little long-term value in them, necessary though they were.

He thought about his conversation with his youngest daughter the day they had put up the Christmas lights on the house. Although they had done the same task for six years before, this year had been different. This year, Mark had realized that the purpose of putting up the lights wasn't so that the house would be decorated. That was just the result of their actions. The real purpose was to give him and his daughter a chance to connect, to find common ground, to share a little more about who they were.

Mark was starting to get better at recognizing the

deeper meaning behind the casual activities of his day. And, he was beginning to choose the hidden purpose rather than just complete the task. Routine tasks became so much more to him. If there was a task in which he couldn't figure out what the deeper purpose was, he made something up instead.

For example, moving the garbage cans to the curb every Tuesday night was no longer just a chore. Instead, he used the time to reflect on parts of his life that needed to be thrown out as well. Old habits, thought patterns, and repeat behaviors were examined to see what value they had. If there was no value, he tossed them out, and chose a new behavior in its place.

The same held true for each activity Mark did. Grocery shopping, cleaning house, driving to church. They all took on new meaning and purpose as he began to live his life in the moment rather than running from the past or trying to avoid the future. Nothing he did felt like an imposition on his time. Although he didn't know it, Mark was setting himself free.

Mark flinched slightly as a stack of papers was dropped in his lap. The teens had completed their assignment and were now waiting for him to respond. He shuffled the papers, mixing up the order in which they were stacked, and then chose one at random and read it out loud.

"Charity is about giving the stuff we don't need to people who need it more," he read, setting the paper to the side and choosing the next one.

"I think charity is when you help other people who need it."

"Charity is what we do at church every Christmas for the homeless."

One after another Mark read the replies. With little variation, they all focused on the task, but not the purpose. Just as he had done for most of his life, these teens looked at charity as something they needed to do, not something they chose to. And when it was done, they moved on to something else. Mark hoped he could find a way to change that tonight, at least for a few of those in the room.

"You all seem to have pretty similar answers here. Charity is something we do to help other people. It's something we have to do, because we would want others to help us if we ever needed it. Would you agree?"

Heads nodded briefly from about half of the participants in the room. The rest simply sat there, looking at him with a blank look in their eyes.

"Well, what if I told you that charity has nothing to do with any of that?" he asked the suddenly attentive room.

A few teens sat up a little straighter, or shifted their position a bit. Some had curious looks on their faces, wondering what he might say next.

"Oh, sure, Jesus told us to feed the poor, clothe the naked, take care of the sick. And we've done that, off and on, for over two-thousand years. So, are we're doing it wrong? I mean, if we've been giving away stuff we don't need, and helping the poor for so long, then why are there still people who need help?"

Mark slowly looked around the room, making eye contact with each teen in turn.

"So, are you saying we're not supposed to help people? That it doesn't really do any good?" Sarah asked him, a look of suspicion on her face.

"Yes, and no," Mark responded, waiting to see how his words might affect the teens.

"Cool!" Tony exclaimed. "I guess I don't need to do that Confirmation service project after all!"

Mark smiled, as did most of the room.

"That's not quite what I'm saying, Tony. Sorry to burst your bubble," Mark replied. "Let me ask you this, who here has done something recently that they would consider charitable?"

A few hands went up.

"Ryan, I think I saw your hand go up first."

"Well, the day after Thanksgiving my family always goes to the homeless shelter downtown. My parents think it's better to help other people than to spend the day shopping," Ryan explained.

"And what do you do while you're there?" Mark asked.

"Mostly just hang out in the kitchen, you know, washing vegetables or cleaning dishes. I can't do any of the cooking 'cause of my age. Then we serve the people."

"Do you spend any time with the homeless while you're there?" Mark inquired.

"Not really," Ryan shared. "They all just come through the line to get their food, then we have to clean up."

"Thanks for sharing, Ryan. Let me ask the group, how many of you would consider this to be an act of charity?"

Hands went up around the room.

"Okay, good. Because it is. And it's not. It is, because Jesus told us to feed the poor, right? But why do you think I would say it's not?"

The room became silent once more. Mark

grinned, glancing down at the floor for a moment. He had two choices here. The first would be to say the answer he had recently discovered. But that wouldn't give the teens the benefit of thinking the situation through like he had done. His second choice was to simply hold on to the silence, to say nothing, to let the uncomfortable sensation of sitting in silence prod the teens into responding. If there was one thing Mark knew about teens, they couldn't stand to be in a vacuum.

Eventually someone would say something. Whether it was a reply to his question, or just random words, he would take the chance to find out. Since Mark was becoming comfortable with silence, he chose the second option. He shifted to a more comfortable position, letting his back lean up against the desk behind him. As he let go of the fear that no one would speak, a shy, timid voice broke through.

"Because, it doesn't fix the problem. It just kinda covers it up?" Zooey asked.

The look on her face made Mark consider that she may have regretted the words as soon as they slipped past her lips. She didn't look like the type to speak out or call attention to herself in any way. She locked eyes with Mark, looking like a deer in the headlights. Her expression begged him to be gentle in his response.

"Interesting analysis, Zooey. Does anyone here agree with her?" Mark said, not yet letting the teen off the hook.

The room filled once more with silence, until, one by one a few hands were raised.

"Justin," Mark said, pointing to a teen dressed almost all in black. "What is it about what Zooey said that you agree with?"

Justin shifted once, then twice before responding.

"Well, it's like you said earlier. Like, there's been homeless people and poor people for thousands of years. People like Ryan and his family have been helping them out all that time, but we just keep getting more. It's like Zooey said, giving them a meal doesn't solve the problem. It just takes care of them for that day."

"I agree," said Victoria. "It doesn't help get them off the street. I mean, it's a good thing to do, but it's not enough."

Mark turned back to Ryan.

"Well, Mr. Ryan? What do you have to say? Was your activity a waste of time?"

Ryan's face twisted as he pondered the question. His eyes looked up towards the ceiling as his hand came to rest on the side of his jaw.

"I don't think it was a waste." Ryan said. "I mean, this one guy that was in the kitchen helping that day, I heard him telling another volunteer about how he was homeless once. He said it was a Thanksgiving dinner just like the one we were serving that he went to when everything changed. He said one of the volunteers sat with him after dinner. The two talked for an hour, maybe more, just about regular stuff. Like life and all that. I guess it made him change how he saw the world or something. Maybe it gave him something to believe in. He said that guy helped get him a place to live and a job. He said the guy stayed in touch with him the whole way, made sure he stuck to the plan and didn't give up. The dude was crying and all. He said it saved his life."

"Ah...that's a perfect example of what I'm talking about. This guy who used to be homeless, why do you think he went to the shelter? Do you think he was looking to change his life?" Mark asked.

"Probably not. He was probably just hungry," Ryan replied.

"I agree. He went there because he was hungry. And, while he was there, was that taken care of for him, or was he still hungry when he left?" Mark continued probing.

"I doubt it. They really fill those plates up good," Ryan said.

"Well, here's where we disagree. And I want everyone to pay attention to this," Mark stated, glancing around the room. "In the first scripture that Robert read earlier, who can recall the final line?"

Mark waited a few long seconds, then reached for the Bible, flipping it open to the first marked page.

"You should rather open your hand, willingly lending enough to meet the need, whatever it may be," he read, paused for a moment, and then repeated, "Whatever it may be. Who can explain how that relates here?"

After only a moment or two, Taylor, one of the younger teens in the room, spoke up.

"Because that guy wasn't just hungry for food. He had bigger needs than just getting something to eat," she said.

"Exactly, Taylor. Good point," Mark explained. "And, I'll tell you guys, this is something that I just figured out myself only a few days ago. Before I started preparing for our session tonight, I thought about charity like most of you shared in your notes. It was just something I did because I felt like I had to.

"I was the kind of guy who would hand someone

whatever change was in my pocket, and then just keep walking. I wouldn't stop to talk or even recognize them. And, you know what? For a few minutes, I might even feel like I did something good for them. But now I see that I never really did help them that much at all. Who thinks they know why it was that I wasn't really helping? Why what I did wasn't really that charitable?"

"Maybe 'cause you can't even buy a taco for less than a buck," Tony said, a vain attempt at humor, which, thankfully, went unrewarded.

"Yeah, that's true," Alyssa shared. "But I think it's more than that. Even if you gave them enough to buy themselves a big lunch, they will be hungry again later."

"Oh, I get it," Robert piped in. "That's what you mean when you said 'whatever it may be', right?"

Mark gave Robert a smile, expressing his approval of what he had just shared.

"Exactly. Like Alyssa said, it didn't solve the problem. It might have been enough for them to get a sandwich, or a cup of coffee, but they are going to be hungry again later. I wasn't helping them find a solution, I was only prolonging the problem. You guys get that?"

Several heads nodded in agreement.

"So, what are we supposed to do then? Not help them? Or help them? I'm kind of getting confused now." Nick stated.

"What does the room think? Should we help them?" Mark asked, raising his hand.

Every hand went up. Mark felt a flush of pride wash over him as he could sense his connection to these teens deepening. Somewhere along the way he had gained their attention, and possibly their respect as well.

"So," he continued to question, "does tossing a

few coins, or providing one meal really help?"

He watched as heads swiveled back and forth. Behind the attentive looks he was receiving, he could see deeper questions beginning to emerge. Rather than continue prodding them to respond, he simply waited in silence, curious to see who might speak aloud the question he felt would come next.

"So, what should we do to help?" Danielle hesitantly questioned.

"More than we do now, that's for sure," said Kayla.

The room returned to silence once more. Mark could tell by the looks in the teen's eyes, the expressions on their faces, they were giving this problem some serious thought. Again, Mark waited. He knew the teens were waiting for him to respond, but something held him back. He felt this moment was far more important than it appeared on the surface. The youth needed to find the answer on their own now. As the silence began to feel uncomfortable, a new thought came to him.

"Has anyone here ever been hungry?" Mark asked the room. "And I don't mean just because you got up late and missed breakfast, or forgot to bring your lunch to school. I mean really, honestly hungry. Like you don't know when your next meal might be?"

Mark watched the room carefully, looking for any sign that someone might want to share, but was afraid to, or perhaps, even worse, ashamed. As he glanced in Kayla's direction, their eyes connected. He could see the struggle going on in her mind, the battle between sharing her experience, which would make her vulnerable to criticism from her peers, or remaining quiet. He silently urged her to share, hoping his eyes would carry his message. He knew how much better it would be for her to let go of the burden she was holding. Slowly, she shifted her gaze towards the floor.

"I have," Kayla shared quietly.

The rest of the room turned their attention to her. No one spoke, and yet, the respect they offered her through their silence was more than enough to give her the courage to share.

"It was three or four years ago. My dad lost his job and we didn't have any money. My mom got a part-time job cleaning houses."

"So you didn't have enough to pay all the bills and buy food, is that right?" Mark asked.

"I guess. Yeah. We had to go stand in line to get free food," Kayla shared, looking up only a moment towards Mark.

"How did that make you feel?" he continued to probe.

Kayla shifted again, crossing her arms against her chest, bending her head even lower.

"Not good," she said, her voice tight.

"Were you embarrassed about it? Or angry? Or just sad?" Mark asked, lowering his voice and softening his tone.

Kayla wiped at her face with her sleeve. This wasn't easy for her to share. Mark wondered if any of the teens in the room knew about this time in her life, or if Kayla and her family had kept it secret.

"I guess sad," she said after another few moments passed, the words barely registering as sound.

Sarah, who was sitting next to her, put her arm around Kayla's shoulders, and then pulled her in close. Kayla gratefully turned towards the safe refuge her friend offered, burying her face against Sarah's sweatshirt. She wrapped her arms around Sarah's waist, holding on tightly as her emotions released.

Mark glanced around the room, sensing the compassion the teens felt for their peer. He waited until Kayla had regained her composure, and then he addressed the room.

"Were any of you in this room aware of what Kayla and her family were going through?" he inquired.

Sarah was the only one to raise her hand.

"We used to bring them food every month, make them meals and such. Our moms have been friends since kindergarten," she explained.

"Okay, so for the rest of you," Mark began, "I want you to think about how hard it must have been for Kayla during that time. As she said, that was three or four years ago, and yet, we can all see how much it still affects her. Think about that last line from the second scripture Robert read earlier.

"'Remember those who are in prison, as though you were in prison with them; those who are being tortured, as though you yourselves were being tortured'. We could add to that, 'remember those who are hungry, as though you yourselves were hungry'.

"This is what I've been hoping you would all understand tonight. You see, when we take action to help someone else, we can't just take the action *we* think is the right action to take. If more of you here had known about Kayla and what she was going through, I'll bet more of you would have helped out. And, sure, Kayla's family would have had more food, and Kayla might not have felt what it was like to be hungry. But, that wouldn't have taken away the embarrassment she felt, or the sadness she carried with her.

"I'm guessing here, but I would anticipate that Kayla probably wanted to do something to help her parents out, but perhaps she wasn't able to. Think about that for a moment. Think about what it would feel like if it had been your parents in that situation, how much you would want to do something to help out, and how upset you might feel if you couldn't."

Kayla interrupted, her voice was hollow.

"Some days my dad wouldn't even eat just to make sure the rest of us had a little bit more. I hated knowing that he sacrificed like that," she shared.

"We can only imagine how tough that must have been for you, Kayla," Mark told her. "And I want you to know I'm very thankful you chose to share that tonight. It might not feel like it, but it helped you more than you might think."

He paused as she looked his way. As their eyes met once more, Mark could tell that it had helped. The struggle he had seen raging inside her just a few minutes ago had passed. Her eyes were more peaceful. He smiled briefly at her. Kayla smiled back, and then she gave Sarah one last hug before letting go.

"Yeah, I do kinda feel better," she admitted, giving Mark another soft smile.

Mark nodded his head.

"For that, I'm glad. And I want you to know that, if you ever need to talk about it more, just let me know, okay?" he offered.

Kayla nodded at him, tears once more forming in her eyes. This time the tears didn't come from pain, but from knowing that someone cared.

"There are two things I want you guys to

remember from tonight, and I have just enough time to share before we close in prayer. First, never stop thinking about what you felt when Sarah shared about her dad's cancer, or when Kayla shared about what her family went through. Realize that everyone you know, everyone you meet or spend time with at school, is more than likely carrying some type of pain or sadness inside. And, just like tonight, you most likely won't know about it, unless they choose to share it. So be kind. Be patient. Show them true charity.

"Charity isn't giving away stuff we no longer need or want because we think someone else might need it. It isn't giving someone just enough to get by for a little longer. It isn't doing only what we feel like doing, or doing something because it will make *us* feel better. That's not charity. That's actually being a little selfish, because we are deciding what we want to do, not giving what they really need.

"Our Catechism tells us that charity comes from our love for God above everything else. It comes from our desire to follow Jesus' words when he said, 'Love one another, even as I have loved you.' Think about if you were homeless. Or if you didn't know when your next meal would come. And then think about how you would want to be treated.

"Would you want someone to just throw some change in your cup, and then walk by without even looking at you? Or would you want them to sit down next to you, and to listen to you as you told them what happened that made you homeless?

"The second thing I want you to remember is the story Ryan shared. Remember that man who had been homeless, who had been living his life in shame.

Remember how the kindness of just one person was all he needed to get back to living a life he could be proud of. He needed someone to listen, to hear him, to help him. Whatever the need.

"Let's make a pledge tonight to live by that motto. Whatever the need. Can we do that?" Mark said, pausing as he watched some of the teens nodding in agreement. "I'll admit, it's risky, though, isn't it? Because then we have to be ready to give them whatever it is that they need and we might not feel capable. But there's one thing we have to remember. We aren't in this alone. You don't have to be the one who fixes everything. You just have to be willing to start the process."

Mark paused, watching for the teens' reactions. He could tell some were still hesitant. A few, though, Mark could see had a passion that was starting to burn. Perhaps they were already thinking of how they could make a real difference.

"And, remember, you can always call me. I took the time to write my phone number on the board behind us. Now, I'll admit, I might not know what to do either, but I'll know where to go for help. Can we make that pledge? Can we become true champions of charity?"

Heads began to nod, and a few verbal acknowledgments sounded as well. Mark could feel the energy in the room as these teens began to see what was possible, to see themselves as part of the solution, and to see themselves as part of a team. They were no longer just a dozen kids who barely knew each other. They had become partners in a noble quest. Mark hoped that the passion they felt would last for a long, long time.

"Then let's plan on meeting together again after the holidays on January 8th, one half-hour before Mass starts. We can meet in the chapel. I'm looking forward to hearing what you all do over the next couple weeks to be a champion of charity.

"Now, we're almost out of time tonight, so let's bow our heads, and, in fact, let's all hold hands as a symbol of our unity tonight. Who wants to offer the prayer?" Mark asked.

Four hands went up right away, and then, everyone in the room had their hand raised. Mark smiled.

"Well then, we'll all pray together," he said.

"Can we pray in a hug circle?" Taylor asked.

"Sure, why not?" Mark responded.

The teens all stood, wrapping their arms around the person on each side, the circle growing tighter as each new member joined. Mark was the final one to join, throwing one arm over Robert's shoulder, and the other over Alyssa.

"Okay, let's take a moment to focus," Mark announced. "Let's remember we're in the presence of angels, and that our Lord is standing here with us right now."

The room took on a more serious tone as Mark led them in the sign of the cross. He then allowed the Holy Spirit to move within the group, letting each teen speak whatever words were in their hearts. They prayed for Sarah and for her father's health. They prayed for Alyssa and for her family. They prayed for the homeless, for the poor, and for those who were lonely or in despair. They prayed for Mark and his recovery, they prayed for each other, and they prayed for the courage to always do what was right.

The group tightened briefly as they ended with a

group hug, and then broke apart. Mark gave one final reminder of their commitment to gather in three weeks before Mass to share their charity experiences with the group, then started to gather the supplies back in their bins.

As the teens filed out, he watched as Robert approached Sarah to apologize for what he had said earlier that night. Sarah opened her arms to give him a hug, which he gratefully received. The two walked out together, their arms tucked around the other's waist, celebrating their newly formed friendship.

Chapter Seven
Reaction

Each one must give as he has decided in his heart, not reluctantly or under compulsion, for God loves a cheerful giver
- 2 Corinthians 9:7

Sunday, January 8

It took a moment for Mark's eyes to adjust to the dim light in the chapel. The only source of illumination came from a red glass votive holder hanging from the wall. The tiny flame inside barely registered as light. The air was still, and cold. He waited another moment while the shadows slowly peeled away, peering into the farthest corners of the room. All he saw were more shadows. Nothing moved. He was alone.

Reaching to his left, his fingers felt along the wall, searching for the switch that would raise the lights. He brought them up slowly, giving his eyes time to adjust, and then stepped towards the center of the room. The chapel was a simple one. Along three of the walls, rows of chairs had been arranged to face towards the center. On the fourth wall, the one furthest from where Mark stood, was the altar. Behind that was the small sacristy where the Holy Eucharist was kept.

Mark checked his watch. He still had fifteen minutes until the time that his group had agreed to meet. He considered using that time to re-arrange the chairs to give the room less of a structured, institutional look, but as he lifted one of the chairs, he changed his mind. Moving enough chairs to create a circle would sap most of his energy. Instead, he simply pushed the first row of chairs in each section back against the row behind, creating a larger open space in the middle of the room.

The floor in the chapel was made from large, hard, Saltillo tile, but the center was covered in a multicolored area rug. Mark figured the rug would provide at least some comfort for the teens to sit or lay upon. It wasn't the best, but it would have to do. He knew he would feel the effects of sitting on the hard surface of the ground far more than the teens would, and so he positioned one chair nearby, just in case he needed it. Mark decided to spend the few minutes he had remaining to ask for help from the one place he knew it would come. He walked to the corner of the room and knelt down on a padded step stationed just in front of the sacristy. Closing his eyes, Mark began to pray.

Mark had become more comfortable with praying in the past few months. Though he still got nervous praying out loud, especially in front of others, when he was alone he found it easier to stay focused if he voiced his prayers out loud.

He would usually start with a memorized prayer, such as the Our Father or Hail Mary, and then simply let his heart speak. Nothing else he had tried brought him greater peace than this. He had begun to relish opportunities such as this when they presented themselves. Kneeling before the Blessed Sacrament was as close as he could come to returning once more to the Throne of God. Ever since that morning when he had woken up in the hospital, Mark found himself craving more experiences like this.

As he prayed, he thought about how much his life had changed, and how much more it may change still. Though, regardless of how often he asked for hints and clues, he still had no idea what God wanted him to do next. Try as he might, he couldn't escape the nagging feeling that he had made the wrong decision the day he quit his job. His youngest daughter had been right. He wasn't someone who was capable of doing nothing. Rather than finding peace, Mark was plagued by a feeling that he was forgetting something, but he could never figure out what that something was. There were definitely still a few pieces missing from this puzzle.

And so, Mark prayed for patience, guidance, and peace. He asked God to help him find the right path. A few bread crumbs along the way, so he would know he was heading in the right direction. That would be nice, too. There was something out there that he was supposed to do. Otherwise, why would God have let him live? Surely he wasn't meant to do nothing. Mark knew the time he spent with the youth was part of the answer, but just how much was what he didn't know. Maybe it wasn't that Mark wasn't ready. Perhaps, he considered, God was still lining everything up. Mark prayed for patience again. He knew he would need it.

A sudden increase in light, followed by a loud clamor made Mark jump slightly.

"Ow," he heard a voice say, "that hurt."

Mark turned abruptly, looking over his shoulder. The door to the chapel was slowly closing, but no one was there.

"I hate when I do that!" the same voice said.

"Who's there?" Mark asked.

"It's Nick, Mr. Counsel," the youth replied.

"Are you okay?" Mark inquired.

"Yeah, I just tripped over my own feet. Don't worry. It happens a lot," Nick informed him.

Mark stood up, walking to where Nick's voice had coming from. As he approached he saw Nick laying sprawled on the tile floor.

"I'm just gonna stay here for now," Nick said, rolling over and putting his hands behind his head. "I'm pretty sure I can't fall down again if I don't get up."

Mark snickered.

"Come on, let me help you," he said, reaching his hand down to assist. "You'll get stepped on lying in front of the door like that."

As if on cue, the chapel door swung open as three teens rushed in. Robert, the first one through the door, narrowly missed stepping on Nick.

"What the heck?" he called out as he lurched quickly to one side.

Kayla wasn't as lucky. She had her head turned, looking behind her as Justin rushed up from behind. Though her first step landed safely between Nick's feet, the next one caught him on the leg. Kayla fell, her hands lunging out in front of her, desperate to grab anything within reach. As her left hand grabbed at Robert's jacket, something flew from her grasp, striking the tile floor. It bounced twice, then slid until it hit a wall.

Nick flinched, trying to twist out of the way, his knee striking Robert on the ankle, causing Robert's already twisting body to lose what little balance he had. As he went down, too, Robert grabbed Mark's outstretched arm. The four ended up in one giant ball on the floor. At first, no one spoke. Then slowly, laughter broke out.

"Now, that right there? That's funny," Alyssa remarked, as she entered the doorway, pointing her cell phone at the jumbled mass of people to snap a few quick pics.

"Oh, that one's getting beaucoup likes!" Justin announced as he too snapped a few pics on his phone.

Robert was the first back on his feet. Still laughing, he reached to help Kayla, and then turned to assist Mark. Nick was already scrambling to his feet on his own. The four stood in a circle holding tightly to the person on each side. Their eyes darted back and forth between the others, and then laughter burst forth again.

"Did anyone see where my phone landed?" Kayla asked as the laughter died down.

"I think it's over against that wall," Robert said, pointing in the direction the phone had traveled.

"It better be okay," Kayla said, "My mom will kill me if I broke the screen again. This would be the fifth time!"

Mark was about to respond when the chapel door opened once more as Tony, Ryan, Sarah, and Taylor entered. In the distance, Mark could see Danielle and Victoria trotting across the parking lot to catch up.

"So, what's so funny? We could hear you guys laughing all the way outside," Tony inquired.

"Oh, you gotta see this," Alyssa said, still playing with her phone. "What's your Twitter?"

"Oh, thank God! Not cracked!" Kayla announced, triumphantly.

Behind him, Mark could hear Taylor teasing the two remaining teens.

"Better hurry! The door is starting to close!" she said as she slowly shut the door.

The two girls were shuffling as fast as they could. They both had huge grins.

"Gah! Hold it open!" Danielle begged as she continued her awkward gait.

"You run like a goober," Taylor teased, closing the door further. The girls giggled even more.

Mark walked to the center of the room and glanced briefly at each of the teens for a moment. Something had changed. He could tell by the way they talked, and the way they teased each other. There hadn't been this much camaraderie the last time the group met. Mark was anxious to find out why.

Taking a seat on the floor, Mark motioned for the others to join him. When they had completed forming the circle and the scattered conversations were beginning to die down, he leaned to his right where Sarah was.

"How's your father?" he asked.

"Still the same, I guess," she replied. "He has good days and bad."

"I've been praying for him," Mark told her.

"Yeah, we all have," she said, nodding to the rest of the group.

Mark could see in her eyes how much she had come to appreciate and care about the teens sitting around her. He had a feeling today's conversation was going to be one that he would remember for a long, long time.

"Okay, we have about thirty minutes until we need to be ready for Mass. Let's start with prayer."

"Zooey isn't here yet," Taylor announced.

"Is she coming?" Mark asked.

"I think so. She told me on Friday she would be here," Taylor replied.

"Okay, we'll give her five more minutes. Can someone send her a text?" Mark asked.

"I got it," Tony said, quickly tapping out a message on his phone.

A few moments later, his phone buzzed. Tony looked down at the screen. His thumbs went into another flurry as he hammered out a reply.

"She's in the parking lot now. Says she's sorry she's late," Tony informed the group.

"Okay, thanks Tony," Mark said, then addressed the entire group. "Why don't we go ahead and prepare ourselves for prayer. We can sit quietly for a few moments until Zooey arrives."

Mark was surprised at the quickness with which the teens responded. Those who had been lying flat shifted into a sitting position as the various conversations floating around the group abruptly ended. Every face in the circle took on a serious look as they bowed their heads, folded their hands in their laps, and simply waited for Mark to begin. A moment later, Zooey entered the room, quietly squeezing into a spot between Alyssa and Ryan.

Mark allowed the moment to linger, feeling a sense of calmness and peace come over the room. As he began leading the teens in the Sign of the Cross, their arms moved in unison. Gone were the casual, nonchalant blessings that he had seen from them in the past. Their movements were purposeful, reverent even. As they recited the Our Father, Mark noted that they spoke clearly and with appropriate volume. They weren't just going through the motions any more. They were honestly praying.

As they completed the closing blessing, making

the sign of the cross once more, Mark paused. The hair on his arms began to tingle, and he sensed that something important was about to occur. Patiently, twelve pairs of eyes reached out to him as the teens waited for him to speak.

"So, who would like to begin? I'm curious to find out what you all have been up to," Mark said, nodding to Zooey as she raised her hand.

"Before we start," Zooey said. "I want to say I'm sorry for being late."

Mark looked at his watch. It was just past five. He figured at least five minutes had gone by during prayer, which meant that everyone had been in the room and ready to go at their agreed upon start time. Although she was the last one to enter the room, he knew Zooey hadn't been late.

"You see, we all said we would get here early today, Mr. Counsel.," Zooey shared. "We said we wanted to make sure we started on time. There's a lot we want to share with you, and, well, I didn't come through on that commitment."

"That's okay, Zooey, we did start on time," Mark said, hoping to dissuade the disappointment he felt from her.

"Yeah, but a commitment is still a commitment. And I didn't keep mine," she replied.

"Well, I forgive you, if that helps. I'm sure the rest of the room will, too. Right?" he glanced around the room.

"Yeah, it was less than two minutes anyway, Zo," Taylor offered.

"Thanks Tay," Zooey said. "But, Mr. C., after the last meeting, me and Taylor were talking. You really

125

made us think, about charity and compassion and all that. We decided we wanted to do something, but like, as a group, not just on our own. So we started texting the others, and before you know it, we had our own little youth group meeting the weekend after Thanksgiving."

"We met for pizza at Bobby's house," Kayla interrupted, "cause, well, his folks have a really, really nice house. Like, you should see the size of his room!"

"It's not that nice," Robert said, an embarrassed look on his face.

"Way better than mine is," Tony interjected.

"And he's got a pool, a hecka nice one with two slides and a waterfall and stuff," Danielle exclaimed. "Pool parties this summer!"

The group shared a laugh, along with a few high fives.

"Anyway," Alyssa said as the celebration subsided, "we spent like, what, I don't know, two or three hours maybe just talking about what we could do to help out. You know, like really help out, and not just do the easy thing. We talked about a food drive, or clothing drive, or something, but everyone else does those this time of year. And that's when Ryan came up with an idea."

"It wasn't really my idea, guys. I keep saying that. It was everyone in the group," Ryan shared.

There was a pause in the conversation as the teens looked from one to another. Mark was anxious. His entire body was buzzing with excited energy and anticipation.

"So? What happened?" he said, reaching his hands out as if he could somehow grab the thoughts in their minds and pull them into his own.

"Okay, okay," Sarah said, smiling at him. "You know how you reminded us that Jesus told us to love one another as he loved us, right?"

"Yeah...?" Mark responded eagerly.

"Well, we started thinking, if most people do stuff because they feel like they're supposed to, then we needed to find something we could do that didn't feel that way. Like, we had to do something that wasn't our idea. Does that make sense?"

"A little," Mark replied.

"Anyway, my grandma lives in one of those retirement homes. And sure, all kinds of groups go there and sing carols for the retirees around the holidays, or help them make crafts and stuff. But we wanted to go there and have them tell us what *they* wanted, what *they* needed, rather than just doing what *we* wanted," Sarah continued.

A look of understanding coming over him, Mark added, "Like it said in that scripture, about 'whatever the need'. That's perfect!"

"Yeah, so, I called and talked to the lady that runs the place and explained what we wanted to do. She was really excited when she understood. Like, she said no one had ever done something like it before. And, Mr. C., it was so much fun! We went back yesterday and did it again!"

"That's awesome," Mark shared, still a bit confused. "Give me the details!"

"Okay, okay, we're getting to that," Tony chimed in. "It was like this. We asked the lady at the place to talk to the people who live there, there's like seven of them, and ask them what used to make them the most happy when they were kids at this time of the year. The old

127

people..."

"We're not supposed to call them that, Tony," Kayla interrupted.

"Oh, yeah. I forgot," Tony replied, "Anyway, the *residents* thought she was just taking a survey or something. But when we got the list, we figured out a way to do everything that was on it!"

"Some of them were pretty tough," Danielle mentioned. "Especially the one with the snow!"

Mark's mind was racing now. He felt just as excited as if he had been there himself. Every face held a smile, every eye glimmered with joy.

"Tell me about that one. What snow?" Mark inquired with an excited smile.

"Okay," Taylor said, "so this guy said his favorite thing to do during the holidays was to make a snowman. He said it always snowed right around Thanksgiving where he lived, and he always made a snowman from the first snowfall. So, we called this place that can make snow and told them what we were doing. At first, they told us how much it would cost, and we were like, there's no way we can afford that."

"Yeah, we were pretty bummed out," Ryan interjected

Mark flashed him a quick smile.

"But then Kayla explained why we were doing it," Taylor continued, "and the next thing you know they volunteered to do it for free! You should have seen the look on the resident's face when he woke up that morning. The entire yard was covered in snow!"

"The guy who said that was what made him happy as a kid, his name is William. Mr. C., you should have seen him. He just cried and cried. He hugged me for like ten minutes or something," Alyssa said.

"What about the others?" Mark inquired. "What was on their list?"

"Oh, most of the rest was simple stuff. Like one lady always had her hair and nails done before Christmas, so me and Kayla did that for her," Sarah explained.

"And another one just loved to go shopping. So I had my mom drive us to the mall and we spent the whole day with her. We had ice cream, and pizza, and just shopped. She only bought one thing the whole day," Taylor said, reaching into her shirt and retrieving a gold necklace with a small charm on it. "It was only like twenty bucks, but she has one just like it, too. She said we're like sisters now."

"Mr. C.," said Sarah, a softer, gentler tone to her voice, "I can't tell you how much we appreciate you challenging us like you did. We would never have thought about doing anything like this before. Heck, we're just kids, right? We're supposed to be lazy and only interested in technology and stuff. Isn't that what the rest of the world says about us?"

There was a brief pause as Sarah was overcome with emotion. The excitement that had permeated the room quickly faded, replaced by a warm glow as each teen's expression reflected what Sarah was trying to say. Seeing that she was struggling to speak, Robert wrapped his arm around her shoulder. She turned towards him, burying her face against his chest.

"We've never had anyone talk to us like they believed in us," Robert continued for her. "Except maybe a coach or something. But that's their job, to get us motivated to *go out there and win*. And for what? So they can have another trophy? That's not going to last. But this, what we did, this was something special. And we owe it to you, Mr. Counsel. You believed we could make a difference. And you taught us to believe we could, too. So, thank you, Mr. C."

"Yeah, thank you," Taylor said.

"Thank you, Mr. C.," echoed Ryan.

One by one the teens shared their thanks with Mark, Mark wanted to say something back, but the words wouldn't come. There was a lump stuck in his throat. He swallowed hard, twice, but couldn't get rid of the feeling. Then his eyes, too, began to water. Never before had he felt so proud. Never had he been so moved, so appreciated, or felt as loved as he did now.

Unable to say or do anything more as his emotions consumed him, Mark simply stood up and held out his arms. The teens rushed in to hug him, those closest to him burying their faces against his coat.

"You guys are the best, you know that?" Mark said as he hugged them back.

"You too, Mr. C.," Taylor said, "you too!"

They stood there for a good long moment, wrapped in each other's arms. Had the church bells not rung out, they might have stayed there for a good moment more. As the sound of bells began to fade, the circle slowly broke apart. Mark noticed that there wasn't a dry eye in the group, especially not his own. He smiled at the teens.

"Before we go into Mass, I just want to tell you how proud I am of you guys. What you did was brave. It took courage. You opened yourselves up and took a huge risk. But you made it happen. And I'm proud of you for that.

"While we're still in the chapel, let's say a quick prayer for those residents you helped, and for all people who don't have someone as daring or as brave as you guys were. And let's pray that teens everywhere recognize their potential, and that they realize how powerful they can be if they just try."

"And, let's pray for more people like Mr. C.!" Tony exclaimed.

As the group wrapped in tightly around him, Mark looked up to the crucifix hanging on the wall behind the altar. Although he couldn't tell for certain, for a moment, he thought he saw the face of Jesus smile.

"I asked for just a bread crumb," Mark silently thought, *"and instead you give me this. Thank you, Jesus, thank you."*

Chapter Eight
Falling

For the righteous falls seven times
and rises again - Proverbs 24:16

Monday, April 10

Mark tossed his bag in the trunk. It landed with a sound that perfectly described his current mood.

'Thump'.

He closed the lid, and then stormed back into the house, hoping to coax Jennifer into moving faster. As he entered, he checked his watch. It felt like the hundredth time that he had done that this morning, and it was only seven-thirty. He was anxious to get on the road. Somehow checking his watch every five minutes made him believe they would not be late. But they were late. Horribly late. So much for wishful thinking.

The destination that awaited them was at least a twelve hour drive. Mark hated checking into hotels at night. He much preferred arriving in the afternoon, which gave him a chance to relax, perhaps catch a quick nap, before heading out to find a place to eat. Instead, they would be lucky to reach their hotel by eight o'clock, leaving him no time to relax. They would throw their suitcases on the bed, leave the unpacking for later, and then rush out to the first restaurant they could find.

He found Jennifer in the bedroom closet, still packing a few last items. Mark could feel his frustration

132

starting to boil. This was the first vacation that they had taken in more than two years, and it was already starting off wrong. He thought about expressing his frustration to Jennifer, but there was no way she wasn't already aware. He had been short with her all morning, responding to her questions with gruff replies. He had also been shutting doors, cabinets and drawers harder than needed and had been wearing a scowl since he woke.

A small voice inside him begged him to let it go, to just relax and remember that everything happens for a reason, but Mark wouldn't listen. He knew he should. He knew that would be the right decision to make, but for whatever reason, today was going to be one of those days. Of course, they could have avoided all of this and chosen to fly instead. There was a ten-fifteen flight that would have landed in Flagstaff by two o'clock, leaving them just under an hour's drive to Sedona. But they hadn't chosen that option. Mark had wanted to drive.

He wished he could go back in time and start over, but that just added to his frustration and anxiety. He knew there was nothing he could do about it now. He knew he was falling into old patterns, but he really didn't care.

"Okay, I think that's everything," Jennifer said as she folded one last sweater. "You're sure it's not supposed to rain while we're there?"

Mark had told her at least a half-dozen times already that the forecast didn't call for rain. He grunted a reply, shaking his head. Jennifer gave him a look that he had come to know really well. She was tired of his ill-tempered responses. Mark turned his head away, ashamed to face his wife. But that just added guilt to the anger, frustration, and disappointment already brewing. Once more the quiet, little voice in his mind begged him to just let it go. At least one part of him knew he was better than he was behaving right now. Still, he shrugged it off, grabbing the suitcase with an aggressive tug.

He could hear his wife saying something as he lumbered down the stairs. What it was that she said, he couldn't tell. His mind was too busy playing out a scenario in which he was verbally giving her hell for not being ready on time. If he wasn't willing to express his feelings openly, then replaying potential conversations over and over again in his mind would just have to do. As the negative patterns continued to take hold, Mark heard that quiet, little voice sigh heavily, giving up the fight.

Mark stormed out of the house, leaving the front door wide open. He lurched across the lawn, reaching for his car keys as he walked. He pulled the keys from his pocket haphazardly, sending them flying across the yard. Frustration boiled over as he tossed Jennifer's bag to the ground and stomped over to retrieve his keys. As he walked back to the vehicle, he saw Jennifer coming out of the house. Mark paid no attention as once more she called out to him. He was far too busy practicing the words his boiling emotions were begging him to say.

Mark pressed the button to release the trunk. Nothing. He pressed it again, still nothing. Angrily, his thumb pressed against it a dozen times, still with no response. With a huge sigh he glanced down at the key fob in his hand. His thumb was on the wrong button. Turning to look over his shoulder, he watched as the garage door finished its upward journey.

"Did you need something from the garage?"

Jennifer asked smugly.

Mark didn't respond. He simply pressed the wrong button one more time, sending the garage door back to the closed position. He then turned toward the car and pressed the correct button. The trunk popped open and slowly rose upward. Mark bent down to pick up Jennifer's bag, not realizing that the trunk door wasn't open fully. He slammed his head against the hard metal edge. The day just kept getting worse.

"Are you okay?" Jennifer asked, feigning a look of concern.

Mark knew she was thinking that he probably deserved hitting his head. In her mind, it was just karma for the way he had been acting all day.

"What do you think?" he shot back.

"Do you need a towel? Or some ice?" she inquired mockingly.

He could tell she was done dealing with his temper tantrum. He knew if he continued, he would be skating on thin ice.

"I need to be on the road already. We're late!" he spat loudly.

Suddenly remembering he was standing outside, Mark looked around to see if any of his neighbors were witnessing his meltdown. No one appeared to be out yet. He reached up and placed his hand on his forehead, checking to see if there was any blood. There wasn't. But he could tell there would be a decent sized bump, and probably a bruise too. Mark reached back down for Jennifer's bag, aggressively tossing it into the trunk. He slammed the trunk down, leaning back to ensure no other body part got in the way.

As he marched around to the driver's door, he

glanced up at Jennifer. She was still standing on the front porch.

"Can we just get in the car?" he pleaded.

"Okay..." she said, half-closing the door. "As long as you're sure you have everything."

"Everything but the three hours we lost by leaving so late!" he shot back.

"Alright, then. I'll set the alarm."

Mark sat down in the driver's seat, giving the seatbelt a rough tug. He started the car, stepping hard on the accelerator. The engine roared loudly, spitting smoke from the exhaust. The passenger door opened, and Jennifer got in. Mark didn't even glance in her direction. He simply put the car in gear and started to drive, fast.

"Jesus! Can you wait until I'm in please?" Jennifer yelled as she grabbed him with her left arm.

Mark glanced over out of the corner of his eye. Her door was still open, one leg dangling out. He hit the brakes, a bit harder than anticipated. Jennifer's body lunged forward, almost striking her head on the dash. She turned towards her husband with fire in her eyes.

"Oh, it's going to be one of these days, then, is it?" she snarled at him.

"I don't know what you're talking about," Mark growled. "Can you just get your seat belt on so we can leave already?"

"You know, Mark," Jennifer said as she reached for her belt, "some days you can be a real child."

Mark hated when she called him that. Mostly because he knew it was true. He was throwing a tantrum like a two-year-old. It had been quite some time since he had a meltdown this bad.

"Okay, I'm in," Jennifer informed him. "We can

go now. Just try to not kill anyone, at least until we're out of our neighborhood," Jennifer goaded.

"Yeah, that's funny..." Mark snarled as once more he pushed the pedal to the floor, the car lurching forward.

They drove in complete silence for the first mile, Mark chewing on his fury like a piece of tough meat. His driving was aggressive, taking turns a bit too fast, and barely slowing down for stop signs. Beside him he could feel Jennifer becoming worried, wondering where the calm, peaceful, gentle husband she had known the last few months had gone. As they reached the end of their neighborhood, Mark turned the car to the right, heading for the freeway onramp.

"We better stop and get gas first," Jennifer mentioned quietly, perhaps not sure she should speak to him yet.

"Well, that's just too bad," Mark replied, glancing at the fuel gauge to see that it was less than half full. "Maybe someone should have stopped and filled up yesterday."

"You do realize that you had the car last night, right? You took it to youth group," Jennifer reminded him.

Once more, she was right, burying Mark even further in his shame. This wasn't the man he wanted to be any longer. It was as if something had a hold of him, something dark and sinister.

"You don't think I remember that? I meant earlier in the day, before I went to youth group. You know I don't like stopping on my way home from church," he said, trying to put the blame back on his wife.

"Um, no, I don't know that. You've never

mentioned that to me before," she replied crisply.

Mark was on the edge of collapsing into a fit of pure rage. He didn't think it was fair that she wasn't taking any of the blame for the delay in their departure. And now she wouldn't take the blame for not filling the tank. He fumed as he drove. In his mind, a silent war was being waged.

"*I can't believe she's so selfish. I would never do anything like this to her,*" one part of his mind offered.

"*Maybe she's right. Maybe she just thought you would fill it on your way back from church. You did pass at least four gas stations along the way,*" the other part shared.

"*But why does she always leave everything to me? Why can't she just figure stuff out on her own? Do I have to explain everything to her?*" part one retorted.

"*You know that's not true. You're just trying to justify your anger now. Let it go! You know this isn't the person you want to be anymore. You really don't want to feel like this, do you?*" part two replied.

"*It's not that easy. She should at least apologize first. Maybe I'll just ignore her and drive the entire way in complete silence. That will annoy the heck out of her. Then maybe she'll feel like crap, like I do now,*" said part one.

"*What would be better, to drag her down into the pit you're wallowing in? Or simply letting go of all this unnecessary negative emotion and just enjoy yourself. You're on vacation for goodness sake!*" part two exclaimed.

"*Yeah, a vacation that's pretty much ruined now, thanks to my wife forgetting to pack last night, and forgetting to fill the gas tank, too. I wonder what else she forgot,*" part one parried.

"*Your morning might not have started off the way you wanted, but, seriously, ruined the whole vacation? You might as well not even go now, right? Why waste the time?"* part two said, flippantly.

Mark thought about it. Why were they going? What was it he had thought was so important that they get out of the house for a while? After all, he still hadn't made a decision about what he was going to do with the rest of his life. He had been out of work for almost five months now. What did he need to take a vacation from?

The answer to that question hit him, hard.

"You're trying to get away from yourself," part two said, the words hitting hard.

It was true. He was running from himself. He was trying to get away from everything that reminded him of his past, everything that reminded him that he had a decision to make, one that he was fighting desperately to avoid. His involvement with the youth group was the only thing that had made any sense, made him feel valued.

But that only lasted for a couple of hours one day each week. With Easter coming up, that meant two full weeks until he would be back with his teens. That was why he had suggested that they take this time and get away. He didn't want to be stuck at home with nothing to do but clean house or work in the yard. The only time he got out of the house was to run errands, or go to church. His anger and frustration wasn't the result of his wife failing to be ready on time, it was a result of the lingering questions he still had. He was just trying to shift the blame to her to keep from having to face his own thoughts. She really didn't deserve the way he had been treating her this morning.

Mark had been feeling a bit off for almost a month now. He wasn't sure what had started it, but something had set his feet back on his old path; feeling worthless, self-doubt, and fear. Perhaps, he considered, the life-changing event he had in the hospital wasn't meant to be a one-and-done scenario. Perhaps that awakening wasn't meant to last the rest of his life. There was still a lot of work to do.

Mark felt his chest relax as he took in a deep, cleansing breath. His eyebrows un-furrowed, and his jaw unclenched. All this time, he had been seeking and praying for the wrong thing. The answer he was looking for wasn't related to how he would spend his time but rather who he needed to become. He had been praying for an easy life but he saw now how unrealistic that was. Life wasn't going to stop throwing challenges his way.

Rather than pray for an easy life, what he really needed to do was to pray for the strength to carry whatever burden he was asked to bear. Yes, he would feel frustrated and angry at times. But he always had a choice. So far this morning, he had wrapped himself up in frustration and anger. Now, though, he decided to make a new choice.

"Jennifer, I'm sorry," Mark said in a gentle voice. "I really am truly sorry."

He could feel his wife start to relax. She took in a deep breath, holding it for a long moment before letting it slide out slowly.

"I am too, Mark. You're right. I could have filled the tank yesterday. I had just as much opportunity to do that as you did. And I could have packed last night, too. I guess, in a way, I wasn't looking forward to this trip. I really didn't want to be on the road at four in the morning. I should have said something, but I didn't. Instead, I sabotaged your plans by not being ready."

"Hon, it's okay. You don't have to apologize. I appreciate it though, I really do. And, to be honest, I wasn't all that keen on leaving so early either. It's just that, well, I suggested it, and you said 'okay', and so we went with it. We really don't need to get to Sedona tonight. The hotel will still be there tomorrow," Mark replied, reaching over to hold his wife's hand. "Look. Let's put this morning behind us. We both know there were things we could have done to prevent what happened, but we didn't do them. I should have shared my feelings with you when I started getting angry rather than let everything build up inside."

"And I could have been more honest," Jennifer explained. "Frankly, I was really looking forward to just relaxing at home. Plus, the fruit trees are starting to bud out. They're going to need to be thinned pretty soon. There was so much I was already planning to get done during spring break."

"Well, I can always take the next exit and head back home if you would prefer," Mark suggested.

Jennifer thought about it a moment.

"No. We're already packed. Besides, you're right, we do need some time away. We haven't had time to just sit and talk with each other for a long, long time now. Let's still go," she answered.

"Okay, but only on one condition," Mark said.

"What's that?" Jennifer asked.

"That we don't let anything else get us down. That we take each moment that comes. Let's not plan out our days. Let's just go with the flow, and let happen whatever happens, okay?"

"You mean, say 'yes' to everything?"

"Yeah. Why not? Maybe there's something we're

meant to do, but we would never think of on our own. Why not let life pursue us?" he replied.

"You know, I kinda like that. It feels way more relaxed than what we normally do on vacation. Yeah, let's try it out and see how it goes."

"Exactly. Somehow I think that's the way we're supposed to live. Like, somewhere in our past we stopped trusting that God would provide everything we need. We started relying on ourselves too much. I don't know." Mark shared.

"You might be right about that. Heck, it's worth a shot!"

"Well, then, first thing we need to do is make sure we have all the resources we might need. How about we stop and get gas and buy some snacks and drinks for the road. We never know where this journey might lead us!"

Jennifer chuckled softly.

"Oh, now you want to stop for gas!" she joked.

Mark laughed.

"Okay, you got me," he replied.

Six hours later, Mark pulled into a truck stop just outside of Barstow for their second fuel stop of the day. He turned to his wife. She was in the middle of a deep sleep, her head cocked to one side, her mouth slightly open. He could hear her breathing slow and deep. He considered not waking her, but his stomach urged him to make this stop a full meal break. He leaned over slowly, running his finger along the line of her jaw.

Jennifer stirred, slowly opening her eyes. As consciousness returned, she wiped the back of her hand across her mouth, and then immediately checked her reflection in the mirror.

"How long was I out?" she asked after taking a long, deep stretch.

"About an hour or so, I guess. I'm not sure exactly when you fell asleep," Mark replied. "We needed to stop for gas, and I really need a restroom. Plus, I'm hungry. I thought maybe this place might have a decent burger or something. You up for getting a bite to eat?"

"Yeah, I could nibble on a little something," she replied.

Mark knew that her 'little something' could wind up being more than he would eat. For a woman who was as fit as she was, his wife could put away an enormous amount of calories.

"Okay, good. Why don't you freshen up and grab us a table. I'll fill the tank, stop by the restroom, and then join you there."

"Sounds like a plan," she said, opening the door and sliding out of the car.

Jennifer took the opportunity to grab one more deep stretch. She reached up as far as she could, and then bent fully at the waist, reaching down to her toes. She put her hands behind her calves and pulled her upper body even closer, her chin nearly touching her leg.

"You always make me jealous when you do that," Mark informed her as he made his way to the passenger side of the car.

"You know I've been trying to get you to come to yoga with me for years. Now that you have so much time on your hands, you really should try it," she said, as she came back to a vertical position, twisting at the waist first to the left and then to the right.

Mark smiled as he watched her walk away. He knew he was really lucky to have such a wonderful woman in his life. Jennifer entered the restaurant, and he turned back to refueling the car. When that was done, he moved the car to a parking spot near the front door. Through the window, he saw Jennifer standing by the cash register, waiting. When he got inside, she informed him the restaurant was pretty full. It was going to be about a fifteen minute wait.

"Restrooms?" he asked.

Jennifer pointed to his left, and Mark headed that way. Upon his return, he found Jennifer talking to another couple who were also waiting. Mark introduced himself, and learned that their names were Steve and Betty Woodson. Steve and Betty were from a town near where Mark and Jennifer lived and were on their way to Phoenix to meet a new grandchild that had just arrived. The four immediately hit it off talking about the joys of being grandparents. The time went by quickly. When the hostess arrived to let Steve and Betty know that their table was ready, Steve invited Mark and Jennifer to join them for lunch. Mark was far hungrier than he thought and readily accepted the offer.

During the meal they continued to talk about their families, different vacations they had taken, and what they did for work. Mark shared that he was on a sabbatical, currently searching for the next big thing. He tried to make it sound more glamorous than it actually was. Towards the end of the meal, Steve asked if Mark or Jennifer had ever been to the London Bridge.

"The actual London Bridge? Or the replica they built in Las Vegas?" Mark inquired.

"No, not that one," Betty began. "The one the Brits tore down years ago. Back when they put up the one they have now. Some rich American decided he wanted the old one, so he bought it and had it shipped over."

"Yeah," chimed in Steve, "they rebuilt it brick by brick just as it had sat over the Thames! The guy that bought it had the workers number each brick as they took them down just so he could put them back up in the same way."

"I can't say I ever even heard of this before, let alone seen it," Mark admitted. "How big is the thing?"

Steve and Betty looked at each other questioningly.

"Heck, I don't recall," Steve said. "But it's gotta be around a thousand feet or so. It's the length of three or four football fields."

"And you can drive over it?" Jennifer asked, her curiosity rising.

"Sure you can. People come from all over the world just to say that they have, too," Betty shared.

"So, what, it's just out there in the desert somewhere?" Mark inquired.

Steve and Betty laughed at the question.

"Oh, no. It's by Lake Havasu," Betty replied.

"Lake Havasu? Where's that?" Mark asked.

"You take the ninety-five south off the forty. It's right on the way. We always stop when we travel this way. Usually we spend the night at this little resort called The Nautical. It's on the south part of the lake." Betty shared.

"Well, they say it's on the lake, but really it's on the Colorado River." Steve explained.

Mark caught Betty give her husband a glaring look. Obviously this disagreement about where the hotel was located had been something they had argued about before.

"You know, it sounds interesting," Mark said, turning to face his wife. "Maybe we can stop on the way back home?"

"Why not follow us? We can show you guys the town, do a little shopping," Betty offered, reaching out and grabbing Jennifer's forearm. "And, Jennifer, there's a darling little art gallery I always stop in when we're there. I'll bet you'd *love* it."

"What do you think, Mark?" Jennifer asked.

Mark looked around the table. The excitement on the faces of Steve and Betty, and the anticipation he saw in his wife's eyes urged him to agree, but his more practical side responded instead.

"You know, it really sounds great. But at the rate we're traveling now, we might not make Sedona until around nine o'clock tonight. If we took a detour, that would add, what, three or four hours to our trip? I've been up since four, so I'm a little anxious to get back on the road."

"Suit yourself. But make sure you find the time to stop on the way home. I guarantee you'll absolutely love the place," Steve said, turning and smiling at his wife. "We always do, don't we, hon?"

Betty giggled, blushing slightly as she did.

"We sure do, darling. We certainly do."

"Well," said Mark, reaching for the bill, "it's been really great meeting you guys, but like I said earlier, I'm a bit anxious to get back on the road."

Mark slid out from the booth, reaching back to help Jennifer as she followed him out.

"Best travels to you then. Maybe we'll see you out on the road coming home," Steve replied, exiting the booth from his side of the table.

"Yeah, that would be great," Mark responded, knowing that the chance of that actually happening was about a billion-to-one.

As they walked to the cashier to pay, Jennifer leaned in close.

"I thought we were going to take life as it comes? Make this trip a grand adventure. You know, say 'yes' to everything. Remember?" she whispered to him.

Mark stopped in his tracks, looking back at his wife.

"You want to make a stop? It's going to add several hours to this already long day of traveling," he explained.

"Well, like you said, you don't like getting into a hotel after dinner, and we've both been awake since early this morning," Jennifer said, convincingly. "Why not see if this Nautical Resort has an available room. I just checked Google Maps, and it's only three hours from where we are now. That would mean we would be checking into the hotel right around four o'clock. Plenty of time for you to take that little nap you always like.

"Plus, these guys seem like they know where to eat, where to shop. We can let them guide us and just go with the flow. Isn't that what we agreed?"

"You know what? You're right. We did," he said, turning around sharply and walking back to where Steve and Betty were still gathering their things at the table.

"You know, Steve, I think we've changed our mind after all. Looks like you guys have some new travel buddies," he said.

"Alright!" Steve exclaimed. "Trust me, you guys aren't going to regret this."

Walking back to his wife, Mark asked, "Can you take care of the bill? I'm going call that hotel to see if they have a room for tonight. And I'll call the hotel in Sedona, too, and cancel tonight's reservation. I'll tell them we will check in tomorrow instead."

Jennifer slid the bill from between his fingers slowly, giving him a sly, sultry smile as she did. He could tell she was already excited about the prospects of this new adventure. And, to be honest, so was he.

Tuesday, April 11

Mark woke peacefully. The morning sun was shining through the partially drawn curtains. He reached for his phone, tapping on the screen to wake it up. It was just past seven-thirty. He stretched, sliding his hand towards the other side of the bed. He felt the warm presence of his wife lying near him. Rolling towards her, Mark wrapped his arm around her waist. Jennifer stirred.

"Good morning, my love," Mark whispered.

His wife grasped his wrist, pulling his embrace even tighter around her. She yawned deeply.

"Good morning," she said. "What time is it?"

"Just past seven-thirty," Mark said. "How'd you sleep?"

"Mmm...really good. You?"

"After the night we had, I slept great!" Mark shared.

"Yeah, that was pretty fun. And to think we almost missed out," she replied.

"I wonder if it was just coincidence, or if there's something to this say 'yes' to everything game we're playing."

"Only one way to find out," Jennifer said.

"Well, then I guess we should get up and go see what this day has waiting for us."

"You go ahead and shower first. I'll see about getting us some breakfast. And definitely coffee."

Mark gave his wife a hug, kissed her on the cheek, and then headed into the bathroom. While he showered, he thought about the events of the past few months, how so much of his life had changed. He thought about all the challenges he had faced, most of which had been brought on by his own negative perceptions. Now that those perceptions were changing, he began to question why he had struggled for so long. There didn't seem to be a purpose to his struggle, at least not one that he could see.

Finished with his shower, he checked his phone for the weather forecast. The report for Lake Havasu predicted a fairly nice day with temperatures peaking in the mid-80s. However, by the time they would be arriving in Sedona, temperatures would be at least twenty degrees cooler. He chose to dress for the cooler temperatures.

As he finished lacing up his shoes, the door opened and Jennifer came in. In one hand she carried a cardboard tray with two large paper cups bearing a familiar green and white logo. In the other hand was a plain, brown paper bag. The smell of coffee reached Mark's senses. His stomach growled.

"There wasn't much to choose from," Jennifer informed him, setting the cardboard tray on top of the dresser. "But I did manage to find a Starbs."

Mark's mouth began to water as he considered

what delicacies might be waiting for him in the brown bag. He reached for the cup Jennifer was handing to him, holding it tightly with both hands. He raised the cup to his nose, cherishing the familiar scent of espresso and spice.

"Is this a cinnamon dolce?" he asked.

Jennifer smiled at him, nodding her head as she dug her hand into the paper bag.

"Nothing but the best on vacation," she said as she pulled out a golden brown pastry. "And a cheese danish, too."

Mark held one hand out to accept the pastry and immediately took a large bite from one end. He chased that down with a long pull from the coffee.

"Oh, that is good," Mark sighed gratefully.

"I thought you would appreciate that," Jennifer remarked.

"You know, it's kinda funny how much better things have been tasting lately. Like, somehow being in a better mood puts more flavor in my food," Mark pondered aloud.

"Maybe you're just learning to appreciate life more," Jennifer suggested.

"I guess," he said. "I've just been wondering why it's taken me so long. Like, why did I have to spend so many years feeling like crap? Why did life have to be such a struggle?"

Jennifer sat down, taking a small bite from her apple bran muffin. Mark could see that she was seriously considering his question. Her eyebrows were clenched together, and her eyes were slightly closed. He took another bite, followed by another drink of his coffee while he waited.

"I guess, maybe in a way, it's like working out," Jennifer shared.

"What do you mean?" Mark inquired.

"Well, remember when you first started lifting weights?"

"Yeah? That was a few years ago."

"Remember how you felt the day after those first few workouts?" she continued.

"Pretty sore. Why?"

"Well, imagine if your life was like your muscles, and God was you, or at least, your mind. And imagine what it would be like if God decided that it was time to strengthen your life. But, your life, just like your muscles, wasn't ready to work out at first. It had to get pulled and stretched first. It had to break down before it could start getting stronger," Jennifer explained.

"Oh, I get it," Mark interrupted. "When I started working out, my muscles didn't know what was happening, only I did. They just knew that they were hurting, but not why."

"Exactly. Just like when God chose to strengthen your life. You just knew it hurt sometimes, but not why you were hurting."

Mark's thoughts drifted as he considered her words. He could see how her analogy fit with his desire to understand his life. It made sense to him that there would need to be some struggle in life in order for a person to grow and develop. Perhaps some people just got the lesson sooner, whereas others took longer, prolonging their struggle that much more.

"Well, for whatever reason, I think my life felt like my legs do the day after lunges," he joked.

Jennifer laughed.

"Another reason why you should learn to stretch!" she exclaimed.

"Okay, okay! I'll come to yoga with you when we get home!"

Jennifer set her coffee down, and what was left of her muffin, and then stood up and held her hand out to him.

"Why wait till we're home? Let's start now!" she suggested.

Mark sighed. He knew he was caught. The 'say yes to everything' plan they were on had put him in a corner this time. He really, really didn't want to start the day trying to stretch, but he knew he couldn't say 'no'. He handed his coffee to Jennifer, and then stuffed the last bite of pastry in his mouth.

"Promise you won't break me?" he joked.

"Come on, silly. You'll be fine. Trust me."

Mark thought for a moment, then said, "I wonder if that's what God has been trying to say to me for all these years?" he mused.

"He probably has, Mark. He probably has," she replied, giving him a loving smile.

Chapter Nine
Release

*My brothers and sisters, whenever you face trials
of any kind, consider it nothing but joy - James 1:2*

Saturday, April 15

"Did you find out what time church is tomorrow?" Jennifer asked from the small balcony of their room.

"Yeah. There's a Mass at eight, and another at ten-thirty," Mark answered from the couch in the main room of their suite. "Any preference for which one you might want to attend?"

"The early one sounds better. That leaves us the rest of the day to ourselves. Tomorrow is our last day here," Jennifer reminded him.

"True. But I've been thinking. I know we have to check out on Monday morning, but we don't really need to go home yet, do we?"

"I guess not. Do you want to stay a little longer?" she asked.

"I don't know. Part of me does, but part wants to get back home too. Maybe we should pack up and start driving after Mass, and then just see what happens along the way. Sound good?"

"Well, that's worked pretty well for us so far," Jennifer admitted.

It was true, too. Each day during their stay their

commitment to say 'yes' to everything had produced at least one experience they might not have otherwise tried. Had it not been for their willingness to be open to life calling them, their vacation might not have been as rewarding as it had been. And it definitely wouldn't have been as adventurous.

They had arrived in Sedona on Tuesday afternoon and had checked in early enough to unpack and still get out for a quick hike before dark. On their way out, Jennifer suggested that they stop by the concierge for other fun ideas, which had led to some of the most daring and memorable activities the two had ever experienced.

On the first day, they took an early morning hot-air balloon ride. While soaring over the famous red rock canyons, Jennifer spotted a group of horses on the ground. So, that afternoon, they took a guided horseback tour. Their guide mentioned that his favorite place to ride horses was on the trails leading into the Grand Canyon. Sure enough, that next morning found Mark and Jennifer boarding a bus for a day trip to the canyon. On the bus ride back to Sedona, Mark overheard a group talking about a hiking photography class they had done a few days ago. As soon as they were back at the hotel, Mark went to the concierge and signed up for a class that was happening that evening, then he had run out and bought two brand new DSLR cameras.

Each day brought at least one new activity that they hadn't done before. From fly fishing one afternoon to renting a tandem bike another, they let the world guide them wherever it would.

Each night after dinner, Jennifer and Mark would take a walk and share quiet time together. When the stars came out and the air got cold, they would huddle close together as they walked, sharing their hopes and dreams about what their future might hold.

Now, on their final night at the hotel, Mark began to dread going back home. A part of him was afraid that being back in the familiar environment would end the adventure they were on. He was fearful that they would return to their old ways and lose the new friendship that they had achieved this week. Curious as to what was keeping his wife busy on the balcony, Mark went to join his wife outside. He wondered how she was able to brave the chill.

"It's freezing out here, babe!" Mark exclaimed, folding his arms across his chest tightly.

"Oh, it's not so bad. There's no wind blowing. Grab a blanket and join me," she said.

Mark stepped back inside and grabbed the extra blanket he had seen in the coat closet. Back on the balcony, he dragged an empty chair as close as he could to Jennifer's, and then sat down, wrapping the blanket around his wife as well. She leaned over, snuggling against him as close as she could.

"You know, I have to tell you, Mark, it's really been nice being around you this week.

"Oh yeah?" he asked. "Why is that?"

"You've just been so much more relaxed, peaceful, and loving. You've been a real gentleman lately, opening doors, holding my chair, and showing true interest in our conversations. It's been like we're dating again."

"I was just thinking about that before I came out here," Mark shared. "And, I have to tell you, I'm kind of nervous."

Jennifer lifted her head off his chest to look at him.

"What about?" she questioned.

"How long this might last," he admitted.

"What do you mean?"

"I don't know. I guess, well, I guess I'm sort of scared that things might go back to the way they were before. Once we're back in familiar surroundings at home."

"You really think so?" she asked, laying her head back against his chest.

"I don't know. I hope not. But I guess if I'm thinking about it now, maybe we should talk things through."

"Sure. What's on your mind?"

Mark paused a moment. He wasn't sure exactly where to start.

"Look, I'll be honest," he began. "Like we talked about before, I really don't like the person I used to be. I'm trying to change, but the meltdown I had on Monday tells me it's not as easy as it seems. I don't think I can just say I want to change, and then, boom, it happens. You know, like how they say you can't teach an old dog new tricks."

Jennifer was quiet for some time. He listened to her breathing while he waited for a response.

"Mark, I want you to know that, when I promised to love you for better or worse, rich or poor, I didn't have any preconceived notions of the type of person I wanted you to be. I didn't have plans for us to live a certain lifestyle, or to have a huge house or fancy cars. If you think we need to make a change, then let's make a change.

"The kids are all grown and moved out now, we really don't need to live in such a big house anymore. We can easily move into a smaller one, maybe even look at one of those communities just for adults. There's one out by the lake that's supposed to have all kinds of activities for people our age. And, just think, we'd probably be the youngest couple in the neighborhood!"

Mark laughed.

"You're probably right about that!" Mark exclaimed. "I've played golf a few times out there. Most of the residents look like they're our parents' age. Riding around in their little golf carts to go to the store, probably playing bingo every Friday night, too. I'm not sure I want *that* much of a change.

"But you are right. We don't need to have such a big house. But do you really want to move? I mean, we raised our family in that house. It's way more than just a place to live now. It's our home. Do you want to leave all those memories behind us?" he asked pensively.

Jennifer was quiet once more.

"I guess not. But we still have a lot of years ahead of us, right? We could make some new memories," she said.

"That's true. Plus, we've always talked about traveling once we had an empty nest. If we did, it might be better to downsize a bit. But, I'm just thinking, I'm not sure how changing the outside environment will help me change on the inside. Sure, I won't be staring at the same four walls every day. I won't be driving the same route to run errands or go shopping. But I'll still be me, wherever we wind up. I think I need to find a way to change what's on the inside, and then, maybe that will make what's on the outside better as well. Does that make sense?"

"Yeah, it does. But, like I said, we didn't get married because I thought you were perfect. Heck, if I was waiting to find the perfect guy, I'd probably still be single!" Jennifer laughed, wrapping her arm around his.

"Well, then why did you marry me?" he asked.

Jennifer looked deep into Mark's eyes.

"Because you were a good person, Mark. I could tell by how you acted when you didn't think anyone was watching. It was the little things you did that made me fall in love with you. Not the gifts you bought, or the exotic trips we took, or how much money you made. It was how you stopped to help people in random places.

"Like this morning, when we walked past that older couple that looked lost. You didn't just point them in the right direction, like most people would probably have done. Instead, you told them to follow you and you walked with them where they were going. That's who you are. You don't just tell people how to get out of the problems they're facing, you get in the mud with them and show them the way out.

"You talk about how you don't like the person you used to be, but I think you're remembering only a part of your past. The person I know, the one I married, he did a lot of good. You helped raise three beautiful children who look up to you. Your kids are proud of who you are. Stop focusing on the parts of you that you don't like. Maybe then you might see what I see, what your kids see. That's why I married you, Mark. And why I'd do it again if you asked me to."

Mark felt his chest tighten. As he looked up at the moon rising over the shadows of the mountains around them, the image became blurry. His eyes felt moist, and an all too familiar lump had begun to form in his throat.

"Maybe Jennifer's right," he thought. *"I've always been a tougher critic on myself than others have been with me. Maybe I haven't given myself enough credit for the good things I've done. I've always shied away from recognition and have had trouble accepting it whenever I've been given an award. Maybe I am a better person than what I'm remembering."*

As he pondered these thoughts, the one question that remained was *how* to change. How could he start being more open to accepting himself? How could he start remembering more of the good things from his past?

"I think you're right, Jen. Maybe I have been too hard on myself. And to be honest, I don't know why. All I know is, at some point in my past, I started playing small. I started believing that I wasn't good enough, strong enough, or smart enough."

Mark paused, feeling the pains of long held wounds rising to the surface. He saw visions of his father disciplining him for doing something wrong. He saw memories of the kids in grade school teasing him for crying when he got hurt. He recalled how he had felt so utterly alone when he moved away to college.

Most of the memories helped Mark see why he had developed such a hard outer shell and had found it so difficult to let others in. His desire to always feel safe had led to an inability to be vulnerable. He had become afraid of being noticed, because if he was never noticed, then he figured no one could hurt him. No one could make him feel ashamed. No one could make him feel afraid.

Mark could feel his chest heaving as his gentle

weeping turned to sobs. He desperately tried to fight back the tears, not wanting Jennifer to know. This wasn't the time to talk to her about what was becoming clear. He needed to face this alone first. Still, as he lost the battle with his grief, she stirred.

"Mark? Are you okay?" she inquired, a concerned tone in her words.

Slowly, Mark stood, gently moving away as he did.

"I'll be back," he said, the words squeaking out tightly.

He walked back into the hotel room, grabbed his warmest jacket, and headed out the front door. With each step, his sorrow threatened to break free. He wouldn't let it. He kept it bottled inside as he marched through the empty hallways. He couldn't risk anyone seeing him in distress, they might ask what was wrong, and he would lose it.

Mark paused just a moment at the elevators, realizing there was a risk of being trapped inside a small box with random people, if only for just a few floors. They would know something was wrong. His eyes were watering profusely now, a fierce grimace was locked on his face. He quickly bypassed the elevators, choosing the solitude of the stairwell instead. There were seven flights of stairs between him and the freedom of the ground floor. His emotions pushed him forward as he raced down the stairs.

As he rounded the corner between the second and third floors, his left foot caught on something unseen, and he slipped. He flew halfway down the stairs, landing in a heap on the floor. His body slid into the corner, his leg pressed at an awkward angle. For a moment his emotional outburst froze as his mind focused on the pain. And then, he screamed.

Both hands grasped at his leg, his body twisting to shift the pressure away from his hip. He rolled over onto his side, curling his leg to his chest. Luckily, the limb still moved. It wasn't dislocated, and it didn't feel broken. He had just taken an awkward, hard fall. As the pain subsided, he stretched his leg straight again, wincing as the bone turned in the socket. There would be a decent bruise come morning.

Mark fought to get his lungs under control. The stress of the emotional overload, coupled with the headlong rush down the stairs and sudden fall had pushed his breathing to the limit. He gulped in air as he struggled to calm down, his breath rasped between clenched teeth, spittle flying with each gasp.

Frustrated, Mark opened his mouth wide, letting a painful moan escape. He rolled his right hand into a ball and slammed his fist against the cold, concrete wall several times, grunting with each strike. Blow after blow landed fiercely, but try as he might, he couldn't pound away that many years of being scared. There was simply too much grief. As his inner pain drove him to tears once more, he pulled himself into a seated position, pressing his back against the wall. He pulled his legs tightly against his chest. There he sat, head buried between his knees, crying out every tear he had ever fought back.

Every vulnerable moment of his past that he had refused to face came rushing back to him. For years these memories had been buried, growing dense with remorse and guilt. They taunted him, jeered at him, and accused him of pretending that they were never real. But they were real. Now, he knew, the time had come to finally face them. Here, huddled in this dimly lit stairwell, curled up against a concrete wall, he was going to set himself free.

Mark cried. At first the tears came freely, like prisoners being released from their cell. They rushed forward, fearful of being drawn back in. Each tear carried with it a memory of a painful time in his past, a moment when he had chosen to cower rather than stand tall. Memories flashed before his eyes, deep secrets burned as they came out into the light.

Like with most things in nature, the strongest ones came first, running headlong towards freedom. They crashed and stumbled over each other, creating a whirlwind of fear, despair, anxiety, and shame. His cries became one long, desperate sob, echoing back and forth through the empty stairwell, growing more mournful with each repeat.

Eventually, only the weakest memories remained. These couldn't rush out, they were too small, too frail. They limped out, treading carefully with each step. His loud, desperate cry faded to a whimper, and then a groan. There was nothing left inside. No tears, no pain, and no fear. It was done.

Sunday, April 16

The sun rose bright and crisp, breaking the horizon just before six o'clock. Mark watched the sky come to life through tired, swollen eyes. His thumb rubbed Jennifer's arm as she slept. Her breathing was relaxed and slow, reflecting how he, too, felt inside. He had emptied himself of so much pain yesterday. All that was left was a calm, gentle, numbness. With his free arm, he rubbed at his tired eyes, thinking back once more to the events of last night.

When he had returned to the room, Mark had found Jennifer sitting on the floor beside the bed, anxiously waiting for him. She took one look at the dirt, sweat, and dried tears on his face, but didn't ask him about it. She simply stretched her arms out wide, her eyes moist with tears, and welcomed him in. He went to her, holding her tight, burying his face in the side of her neck. He held her close as she cried for him. He wanted to cry with her, but he had run out of tears.

When she was done crying, he helped her into bed, then sat down next to her and started talking. For hours he shared with her every part of his past, every painful memory. He told her of his fears, doubts, and despair. Jennifer listened attentively, only asking questions to let him know that she understood what he said. She didn't judge, she didn't try to fix things or placate him in any way. She gave him her full attention. She gave him her heart.

When he said all he could, she curled up against his chest, told him how much she loved him, and then drifted to sleep. But not Mark. Sleep didn't come for him. The emptiness that remained wouldn't allow him the comfort of sleep. Throughout the night his thoughts churned, trying to decide what to do next, now that he no longer felt afraid. It was as if he had been reborn. A suitable feeling, he considered. Today was Easter, after all.

Mark thought that moments like these were supposed to bring clarity, the unfolding of life's greatest mysteries. All he felt was empty. He was the proverbial blank canvas, an empty page begging for words. He knew there was still work left to do, but at least he would be starting anew.

Beside him, Jennifer stirred. Her eyes began to flicker, her breathing became less deep. The morning sun was just starting to peek through the bedroom curtains. Mark shifted his body ever so slightly, hoping to remove his arm from around her shoulders without waking her further. If he couldn't find the rest his mind and body so desperately needed, then at least he would ensure she found hers.

Slowly, Mark moved his arm, holding Jennifer's head with his other hand. When he had moved his arm far enough, he lay her head gently back down, then inched his body towards the side of the bed. Pausing to glance back at his wife, he stood up, a warm smile on his face. Still looking in her direction, he moved towards the bathroom, hoping to grab a shower before she woke. Not paying attention to where he was going, his foot caught the edge of the comforter, and he stumbled. His right hand grasped at Jennifer's vanity case, sending it crashing to the floor. Makeup and hair accessories scattered in every direction.

Jennifer shot up in bed, her eyes wide open. Her head swiveled rapidly, trying to find the source of the noise. Finally, her eyes fixed on the spot where Mark lay sprawled on the floor.

"Oh my God, Mark, are you okay?" she blurted out, jumping off the bed to rush to his side.

"Yeah," Mark groaned. "I just fell. Pulled your makeup bag down with me. I hope nothing's broken. I mean your makeup, not me."

The look of panic on Jennifer's face faded.

"Oh, honey, you look terrible," she said as her

eyes glanced over his face. "How much sleep did you get?"

"Sleep?" he asked jovially. "What's that?"

"Have you been up all night?"

"My mind just won't slow down," Mark said, nodding his head. "I know I'm exhausted. I can feel every part of my body begging for sleep, but I just can't turn off this flood of thoughts."

Jennifer sighed, taking a seat on the floor next to where Mark had fallen. She ran her hand along his arm, her eyes locked on his.

"What can I do to help?" she asked.

Mark shrugged.

"I don't know. That's the thing. It's like, after everything I went through last night, instead of being filled with answers, I'm filled with even more questions."

Jennifer wrapped her arm around him and pulled him in close.

"I don't know, babe. I wish I had all the answers for you. But I don't," she told him.

Mark sighed deeply.

"Maybe no one does..." he thought.

A feeling of sadness began to creep over him, causing his throat to tighten again. Fighting off the sorrow, he reached up and grabbed Jennifer's arm, pulling himself out of her embrace.

"Come on," he said, reaching down to help Jennifer to her feet, "let's get ready and head into town. I want to get an early start today."

"Are we going to come back to the hotel?" she asked, starting to pick up the items scattered on the floor.

Mark paused, his brows furrowing as he considered.

"I don't think so. We should have time to check out before we head to church. Then I think we should just grab a bite and just start driving."

"Are we heading home?"

Mark looked at his wife. She was clearly wondering how he would be able to drive all day having had no sleep.

Mark sighed as he walked away, "Honestly, I really don't know."

Chapter Ten
Exploration

*I love those who love me, and those who
seek me diligently find me - Proverbs 8:17*

Saturday, July 15

Mark paused a moment at the top of the hill, reaching behind his back to retrieve his water bottle. The morning sun was already blazing. After taking a long drink from the bottle, he removed his baseball cap and wiped his arm across his forehead. He poured some water into the cap and let it soak through, and then placed the cap back on his head, relishing the cool sensation.

Mark returned the water bottle to the side pocket of his backpack. Twisting to the other side, he fished through another pocket to retrieve his phone. The glare of the sun made the screen hard to see, which forced Mark to turn his body until the phone was in his shadow. He opened the maps application and checked his position. It showed just over two miles remained. He sighed deeply. It had been quite a few years since he had last hiked this trail. He didn't remember it having taken this long, or having been this exhausting. Then again, the last time he was out here was before he proposed to Jennifer. Mark was still a young man back then.

Looking around, he was amazed at how

everything still looked the same and yet, somehow, it was all so different. Each landmark he passed raised new questions in his mind.

"Is this the tree I had almost fallen out of?"

"Is that the rock where I caught the snake?"

"Could that be where I camped one winter?"

The questions paraded by, forcing distant memories into the open like strangers appearing from a fog. Mark turned back in the direction he needed to travel, twisting once more to place the phone back in its pouch. He then placed the edge of his hand against the bill of his cap to shade his eyes and stared into the distance.

"Two more miles, in this heat? What on earth was I thinking?" he wondered, shaking his head at his own foolishness.

Adjusting his backpack to ride more comfortably on his shoulders, which were already beginning to complain and chafe, Mark resumed his lumbering stride. Even though he didn't quite understand why he had decided to start this hike on such a warm day, he felt he was being guided to come out here. It wasn't a reason he would find with logic, which meant it had to come from faith.

"I remember being able to finish this hike in under three hours," he whispered to the grass around him as he turned his attention back to his hike.

But the grass didn't answer. They just stood there, looking as dry and thirsty as he felt. He had been walking now for nearly four hours. Mark brushed his hand across the tops of the grass and then twisted off a few of the pods. He split one open, put the seed between his teeth and bit down. He spit the cracked seed into his palm and turned the two halves over a few times. He had done this same thing a hundred times in his youth. Yet, he had never been able to see the plant that waited inside. He knew the seed held a secret. One day it would become next year's grass. But how it did that was a secret the seed would tell no one until it was time.

Mark tossed the remaining seeds into the breeze, and then wiped his palm on the leg of his shorts. He had reached the bottom of the hill, and, with a few more steps, would be climbing the next. Though every hill appeared similar to the last, each new climb felt steeper. Although, he considered, that was just the result of tired limbs. He made a mental note to exercise more frequently.

For the next forty minutes, Mark ascended one side of a hill and then lumbered down the other side. Finally, he reached a point where he could see the valley. The final hills between him and his destination lay just ahead. His pace quickened in anticipation, longing to be in the shade of the small building that had been so many things to him in his youth.

At one time, many years before he had been born, the building had been a railway station, serving a town that no longer stood. All that was left was the old brick building. But to the playful imagination of a young boy, the station had transformed into so many things. A machine gun nest in World War II, a jailhouse from the old west, a bank just waiting to be robbed. It was even an alien dwelling once, on a planet yet to be discovered.

As those memories flashed through his mind, Mark reminded himself that there was one other reason he used to come here. It was a place to hide from the world. When the troubles of his youth became too much to handle, this is where he would come to breathe and think. At night, the quiet and abundance of stars had helped him set aside his worries.

Mark smiled. He had forgotten about that feeling of protection, as if he had been safer out here in this valley than any other place on earth. He silently prayed that he would find that feeling again. Peace. It was something that was desperately missing from his life.

Coming to the top of the last hill, Mark looked down into the valley below. There, right where it should be, was the station. From this modest height, he could see where the tracks entered the valley on one side, and where they disappeared on the other. Mark had never walked those tracks, not for long, anyway. He still had no idea where they came from, or where they were going. He only knew they were there.

From the distance, the old building looked different. Darker than he remembered, and more worn down. It appeared to list to one side, like his father did, coming home late on Friday nights. He began to wonder if the building would still be safe enough to enter. He hoped that it would be. It was the only shade he would find out here for miles. Nothing in this valley grew that reached higher than his knees. If he was to escape the worst of the afternoon heat, the cooler temperatures inside the railway station would be his only hope.

Walking more carefully now, Mark left the wispy grass behind and wound his way between the scrub and tumbleweeds of the valley floor. Splashes of dull yellow speckled the dingy gray and dusty tan that permeated the area. The only greenery he could see was in these last few mustard plants still protesting the onset of summer. Winter was their domain, when the entire valley shouted with color. Mark had been witness to that display, marveling at how alive this normally drab and desolate vale could be.

As he picked his way through the scrub, his mind was drawn back in time. Six weeks ago, he had participated in the final youth ministry program for the school year. It was also the time of year when Jennifer was at her busiest with report cards, conferences, and packing up her classroom for the summer. Mark had found himself alone and with nothing to occupy himself for far too many hours each day. The questions he had been able to avoid for months were now looming over him. It was time to decide what he was going to do with the rest of his life.

One thing he knew for certain was that he would do his best to not waste any of it. Whatever he chose to do would be something of value. Since he hadn't made a trip back to visit his folks in a while, it just made sense to make up for that now. And, once he arrived, he had an unmistakable urge to visit his old stomping grounds. A quick trip to the local camping store yesterday provided him with everything he needed.

Today, he had woken up at dawn, and just started walking. Now, looking up to get his bearings, Mark froze in his tracks. Graffiti. The reason why the building had looked so much darker from the top of that hill earlier was glaringly apparent now. At some point since his last visit out here, someone else had stumbled on his old hangout. Hateful and crude words marred the surface. Vulgar images stared back at him, making his stomach turn. Mark tried to turn away. He didn't want to continue looking, but the shock of finding his old hideout branded in such distaste held his gaze. His emotions bubbled and boiled. Sadness, anger, frustration, and defeat all mixed together in a sour, acidic blend.

Mark tried to swallow but his mouth was dry. He had to get out of the heat. Moving slowly now, he made his way to the front of the building and then paused at the door. Praying he would find that the inside had not been vandalized the same as the outside had been, he cautiously pushed the door open. He stepped as close as he could to the threshold but did not dare enter in. As his eyes adjusted to the dusty gloom, he saw that the inside was not anything like the outside. It was worse.

The floor was covered with shards of broken glass bottles, smashed soda cans, and crumpled food wrappers. In the center of the room, the floor had been charred where a makeshift fire pit had been built. The ceiling above was dark with soot. On every wall hung pictures of women. Some had very little clothing. Most of them had none. The room smelled of smoke and sweat.

Mark stood in the doorway, no longer wanting to enter. Here, in the same building where he had once sentenced the imaginary bandit One-Eyed Joe to jail for one hundred years, there now hung the faded, torn remnants of some other young boys' much darker fantasies. With a heavy, mournful sigh, Mark turned around and walked away. He took a few steps, then stopped, the building at his back. Shaking his head, he spat out his disappointment and anger. He knew he could no longer hold memories from the playful days of his youth without this new memory to plague him. The vandals had not just damaged the building. They had damaged his past.

Mark breathed in deeply and then let out a long, angry growl. He looked for a rock. Not a big one, just one large enough to kick. With none to be found, he tried kicking the dust, but it barely made a cloud. Searching for something to take his frustrations away, Mark walked until he reached the edge of the tracks. There were a lot of rocks here. The tracks sat on a bed of them. None of the rocks were big enough for what he wanted to do, however.

"What now? Was I brought out here just to see this?" he asked the emptiness around him.

His plan had been to spend the warmest part of the day in the station, out of the sun. Just sitting, thinking, and reflecting. But he couldn't do that now. Even if he tried to clean it out, the taint would still be there. There was no way he could be inside that building with a clear mind. He would have to find some other way to spend the day. Otherwise, he would need to make a five-hour trek back to his parent's. He didn't think his legs were up for that.

Turning back for one more glance at the station, Mark again spat upon the ground. He then turned to his right and looked down the tracks as far as he could. Seeing nothing there but more dirt and scrub, he turned around and looked the other direction. He hoped there would be a sign standing out along the tracks that would lead him to choose one direction over the other. There was nothing.

Closing his eyes, Mark fought back the tears. His deep disappointment had turned into unrestrained frustration. His hands closed into fists, his shoulders tightened, and his jaw clamped down hard. His shallow breathing dragged between clenched teeth, making a hissing sound. Panicking now, Mark turned from left to right, searching desperately again and again for any sign of what to do next. Again, nothing spoke to him. Still, he couldn't escape the feeling that he was here for a reason.

With a moan of defeat, Mark fell to his knees, casting his eyes to heaven. He cried out hoarsely.

"What do you want from me, God? I know you brought me here for a reason. I know you are guiding me. I just don't know why. You told me you don't want me, not as I was. But who am I supposed to be? What am I supposed to become? I have changed so much already, what more am I to do?

"Did you bring me out here just to experience more pain? Just for me to see the memories of my youth callously destroyed? I've let go of so much I didn't need these past few months. I've surrendered almost everything I have. Do I need to lose my past now, too? I don't understand, God. I honestly just don't understand."

Mark bowed his head, fighting to stay in control. The feelings that gripped him now were dark and ugly. He didn't want these thoughts. Not again. Years ago he had felt despair like this, and it had almost cost him his life. Mark knew there was only one thing that would help. Prayer.

Struggling against the turmoil, he slowly relaxed. His hands loosened and then his shoulders fell. He began to hold each breath as long as he could and then let it out with a long sigh. Mark was feeling his body relax more and more. This time, he wasn't going to give in to despair. This time, he would remain strong. Slowly, Mark got to his feet.

He glanced once more in each direction, then

clasped his hands, bowed his head, and began to whisper out a prayer.

"Heavenly Father, I may not understand what it is that you want from me. I may not understand why I have had to let go of so much of who I am. But, if it is your will, then I surrender it now. I give up my desire to control, to decide, to choose. I give my life fully to you now. Please, tell me what it is you want. Wherever you send me, I will go. Just, please, give me a sign. Show me the way. I will follow. I will."

Just then, a cool breeze danced across Mark's face. Opening his eyes, he looked in the direction the wind had come from. To his astonishment, clouds were hastily forming on the horizon. White billows grew and blossomed, covering the once clear, sapphire sky. Tighter the clouds bunched, changing from white to gray. Mark stood, statuesque, a look of wonder and awe etched on his face.

And then, a mere moment after the last spot of blue was swallowed behind the curtain of clouds, a single ray of sunlight broke through. It beamed down upon the earth, coming to rest around one of the telephone poles that ran along each side of the track. The way it shone reminded Mark of paintings he had seen of a cross with a white garment draped across it and a single sun beam shining down.

"This can't be a coincidence," Mark said out loud to the rocks and plants, and then paused a moment, as if they would respond.

With bold determination, he took one step, and then another, moving slowly in the direction of the light. As he drew near, the clouds shifted and the beam disappeared. Mark paused, wondering what might happen next. A moment later, further down the track, a new ray shone through, once more changing a common telephone pole into the image of a cross. Mark began to walk faster now, his confidence growing with each step.

He had no doubt, God was calling him. It no longer mattered why he was being called, or what he was being called to do. Mark began to smile, and then he began to laugh. His slow, plodding pace quickened. His feet felt as light as air. He knew now that his past no longer mattered, only his future. And that, he knew, would from this day forward be a life that belonged to God.

Chapter Eleven
Resurrection

*And without faith it is impossible to please him, for whoever
would draw near to God must believe that he exists and that he
rewards those who seek him - Hebrews 11:6*

Thursday, July 20

Flakes of dust flickered as they floated in and out
of the light shining through the small window. Mark
watched as the flakes danced, played, and fell gracefully
to the floor. Looking at the furnishings around him, he
would have thought that this room was impervious to
dust. There wasn't a single piece of furniture that looked
anything but immaculate. Tabletops, lamp and plant
stands, book shelves and wall hangings all appeared
shielded from the dust falling through the room.

Mark sat on a black leather couch. The cushions
seemed to melt under his weight, so that he was more
embraced by the sofa than he was sitting on it. Across
from him, Father Kevin sat in a large, padded leather
chair. He had both feet on the floor, and was sitting in a
position that made Mark feel that whatever he had to say
was important. They had just finished praying together.

Mark began the conversation casually by talking
about his experiences as a youth group volunteer. He
shared some of the insights he had gained, and
conversations he had recently had with the teens. He
then talked about his vacation to Sedona, starting with

his meltdown on that first morning and the agreement to say yes to everything.

He explained how it had seemed that all of the activities they were involved in had come to them, rather than Mark or his wife planning them. Father Kevin commented on how close their experiences resembled God's grace. He explained how blessings and miracles were always available to those who were open and ready to receive. Father Kevin then told him how God is always sending us everything we need, but because it isn't wrapped in the packages like we were expecting, most people walk right past exactly what they prayed for without even knowing it.

When Mark began to talk about his experience in the hotel stairwell, and the deep conversations he had had with Jennifer on their final night in Sedona, Father Kevin listened intently and allowed Mark to finish entirely before speaking. When he did finally speak, his words were soft and gentle, reflecting the compassion Father Kevin always had in his eyes.

"It may sound strange to you, Mark," Father Kevin began, "but I'm actually glad you had an experience such as you describe."

Mark looked at the priest with a surprised and somewhat nervous expression.

"Can I ask why?" he asked slowly.

Father Kevin smiled, his eyes locking on to Mark's, his hands resting on his knees.

"Ecclesiastes, chapter three, gives us the well-known scripture that says, *'There is a time for everything, and a season for every activity under the heavens: a time to be born and a time to die, a time to plant and a time to uproot...'* and so on. What you experienced was the *uprooting* of your past. Like when a farmer plows a new field, removing all the rocks and roots that would keep his crops from growing. Our lives, too, have their cycles."

Father Kevin leaned in closer and lowered his voice even more.

"What it means, my nervous friend, is that you are being prepared for growth. God brought you to a place where you were able to clear out a patch of new soil inside you. Now that you've done the work of eliminating your attachment to the pain that made you feel stuck in life, you are free to take on what God will ask of you next."

"Huh..." Mark grunted. "That reminds me of my experience on the railroad tracks."

A soft chime sounded from outside the room. Father Kevin frowned, and then sat back, glancing quickly at his watch.

"I'm very curious to hear about that. But I'm afraid that was the doorbell. My next appointment has arrived," Father Kevin said as he stood up and placed his hand on Mark's shoulder.

"Tell you what. Let me see if I can reschedule. It's just a budget review. Nothing that can't be done a little later this afternoon. I don't want to leave this conversation half complete."

The tension in Mark's shoulders released and a more relaxed look came over his face.

"I'll be right back," Father Kevin promised.

Mark sat in silence, once more watching the dust flakes flicker in the light. He took some time to browse the wide assortment of books on Father Kevin's shelves, finding topics ranging from botany to transcendental meditation. He spotted a book on Buddhist philosophy, copies of the Bhagavad Gita, the Koran, the Tao and other eastern religious doctrines mixed in with dozens of books stating more Christian oriented themes. Mark wondered how many of the books Father Kevin had actually read, and how many had found their way to his shelves as gifts from parishioners or friends.

Mark grabbed three books at random, and then returned to his place on the couch, quickly glancing at the titles in his hand. The first, titled *The Phenomenon of Man,* was wrapped in a baby blue cover with a white omega symbol on the front. The book was written by Pierre Teilhard de Chardin. The next book had a full-color photograph of the Dalai Lama and was titled *The Art of Happiness.* The final one had cartoon graphics of whirling dervish dancers along with the title *The Masnavi: Book One* by an author known simply as Rumi. Mark had never heard of any of these titles, and, other than a passing knowledge of the Dalai Lama, didn't know much about the authors either.

As Mark arranged the three books on the couch next to him, the dark walnut door to Father Kevin's office opened with the slightest squeak. Father Kevin paused at the threshold a moment with a peaceful, relaxed look on his face. He stepped softly across the floor, smiling gently as he re-entered the room. Taking his place in the chair across from the couch, he glanced at the books Mark had placed next to him on the couch.

"You found some interesting titles there," Father Kevin mentioned casually.

"To be honest, I grabbed them at random from the shelf," Mark explained. "You sure have an extensive and diverse collection of reading material. Have you actually read all of these?"

"Almost. The three you pulled out, yes. But this shelf on the bottom," he said, pointing to the shelf closest to his chair, "holds the books I'm currently reading, and the ones still waiting for me to begin."

"I admit, I'm curious about some of these titles. Don't they express values and opinions opposite to our faith?" Mark looked inquisitively at Father Kevin.

"Perhaps *opposite* isn't the best word," Father Kevin responded. "If you take the time to truly understand the underlying philosophy of each of these books, you will see that there are values strongly related to Christian doctrine woven throughout. Most of the books with more eastern philosophies were ones that I read during my days in the seminary. I took several classes on world religions."

"Really? Why was that?"

Father Kevin shrugged slightly.

"How could I ever argue the merits of Catholicism if I don't truly understand how it compares? How could I make the decision to devote my life to living and teaching our faith if I knew nothing more than what our Catechism describes?"

He paused a moment, his head turning slightly to the side, drawing Mark's attention further.

"Have you ever made a significant decision, which could change the course of your future, without weighing all possibilities?" Father Kevin asked.

Mark could think of only a few times in his life when he felt that he had made a life-altering decision. The day he chose his major in college, the day he proposed to Jennifer, and the day they first decided to start a family. In each of those moments, his contemplation had been fairly extensive. He realized that the decisions he had made were far more personal, and affected a much smaller audience than the one Father Kevin had made. Father Kevin not only changed his own future, he had also moved into a position where he was capable of affecting the lives of thousands.

"So, you're saying that these books influenced you to become a priest?" Mark asked.

"Influenced? Maybe. More like they validated. I didn't choose Catholicism solely because I disagreed with all other doctrines. It was more that, after having chosen Catholicism, I tried to find any reason I could to change my mind. Instead, everything I read here helped me see how perfectly our faith fits with my personal values and beliefs."

"I'm not sure I understand," Mark admitted. "You mean you weren't raised Catholic?"

"No, I wasn't. My father claimed to be an atheist, although I think he was more agnostic. And my mother, well, let's just say she was a *free spirit*. She's the reason I read *Autobiography of a Yogi*," Father Kevin shared, reaching for a book on the shelf behind him.

"What's that one about?" Mark inquired.

"Tell you what," Father Kevin said as he offered the book to Mark, "why don't you add it to the three you have now? It's probably best if you discovered what it's about for yourself rather than be influenced by my perceptions."

"I'm not sure that I was planning on reading these," Mark mentioned, pointing to the three books already by his side. "In fact, I'm still not one-hundred percent sure why I grabbed them in the first place."

"Well, you couldn't have chosen three better books to guide you through the next step in your journey," Father Kevin said, still holding the fourth book in his hand. "And, with this final one, I think you'll find your current question will be already answered."

"Which question are you referring to?" Mark asked, reaching out to take the offered book.

"The one you haven't asked yet," Father Kevin said with a knowing look on his face.

Mark tilted his head to one side and looked at the priest from the corner of his eye.

"Does he really know what I'm thinking?" he wondered in silence, *"Or is he just making a guess?"*

"You mean, what I'm supposed to do next?"

"Yes. That's the one. But first, tell me about this experience you had. Something about a railroad? The look on your face when you first said it tells me it was a powerful experience."

Mark breathed in deeply, and then sighed.

"Yeah, you could say that. Although, to be honest, I'm having a little difficulty believing it myself. It was, I'm not sure how to describe it. Magical, maybe? It was definitely strange."

Father Kevin chuckled comfortably, further reducing the stress Mark felt.

"Well, you don't need to worry about telling me. I'm a firm believer in miracles and mystical encounters with the Divine," Father Kevin said casually.

His tone assured Mark that his words were earnest and true. Shaking his head slightly, as if to clear it of any lingering fear, Mark began. He told Father Kevin about the railway station, about how much it had meant to him in his younger days. He told him how he had recently returned and had found it damaged, and how difficult that had been for him, as though he was losing one more part of himself. He told him about how he cried out to God and had asked Him why it seemed He was taking away everything Mark had been familiar with. He said he had begged God to give him a sign. Mark explained how the sky had grown cloudy and how light had broken through to surround the telephone pole. He described how the light would move to another pole further down the tracks as Mark drew near. Then, Mark became silent and slouched a little on the couch as if anticipating a negative response.

At first, Father Kevin said nothing. He simply looked at Mark with eyes that shone and glimmered. Then, he sat back, gently nodding his head as he smiled.

"So," he said with a gentleness that instantly relieved Mark's concerns, "you might not realize it, but that day, Mark, you walked where angels dwell. It is definitely a sign that our Lord is preparing you for great responsibility in His kingdom. May I ask what happened next? How long did the experience last?"

"I walked for, I don't know how long, maybe a couple of hours? Maybe longer."

"And what happened after?"

"The railroad eventually crossed a road, well, more like a dirt path. The sun beams stopped shining, and the clouds began to disappear. And then, I understood that I was meant to follow the road. So, I did. I walked for another hour or so before I came to a gate, like the ones they use to block off the highways up in the mountains during winter. You know the kind I'm talking about?"

"Yes, I do. So, what happened then?" Father Kevin asked, nodding his head once more.

"Well, there wasn't a fence or anything, just the

gate, so I just walked around it. It must be there just to keep people from driving past it. The road on the other side of the gate was paved. That's when I called you, when I got to the paved part of the road. Something inside me told me I had to set this appointment as soon as I could, to meet with you right away," Mark shared, glancing up tentatively at Father Kevin as he waited for a reply.

"So, that's why you sounded so anxious. That makes sense now," Father Kevin said, nodding his head. "And, that was it? You just had a feeling that you should call me? Nothing more?"

"No, not that I *should* call you," Mark answered slowly, closing his eyes slightly, "that I *needed to* call. Like, it was the next piece that fit in this puzzle. I don't know how to explain it better than that. Does that make any sense?"

"Oh, it definitely does. And, I believe I have something that will help you. But first, let me share with you something that I've learned partly through my reading," Father Kevin said as he waved his hands towards his books, "and partly through my experiences working with people going through life-changing experiences very similar to yours."

"Anything you can share with me that might help, I'm all ears."

Father Kevin smiled, folded his hands in his lap, and then sat back more fully into his chair.

"Everyone who enters into a spiritual quest, like the one you began in the hospital, eventually realizes one thing. The quest is not about finding answers, it's about finding the right questions. The answer you seek isn't *out there* somewhere. You'll never find it by looking for it."

"I'm not sure I follow," Mark interrupted. "Do you mean that the question I have isn't the right question, or that it doesn't have an answer?"

"A little of both, I guess," Father Kevin said. "Look at it this way. When you ask a question, you expect to find an answer, right? Isn't that the way we're taught in school?"

Mark nodded in agreement.

"We're asked a question, and then we try to find the right answer. But life isn't like science or math, or even like religion for that matter. Life is spiritual, experiential, not logical or structured. In life, the questions themselves *are* the answer. Where you are now isn't a question that needs to be solved. It's an answer that needs to find the right question."

"You kind of lost me there," Mark admitted, looking a bit confused.

Father Kevin smiled again. The look on his face told Mark that he wasn't the first person to have difficulty understanding this philosophy.

"You believe that your experiences – the hospital stay, the revelations you've had, this spiritual encounter, even that meltdown you told me about – are all pointing you in a certain direction. You believe that they are there to give you a place to start from, a jumping off point to uncover your purpose in life, correct?" Father Kevin asked.

"Yeah, I guess. What are they really for then, if not to generate a new way of looking at life?"

"Exactly my point! You are already looking at life differently. You've reached a point where you understand that your life has changed somehow. You think the changes are meant for you to find an answer, but they won't, because *they are* the answer. You've been exposed to the answer you need. You already know what you are supposed to do. But you won't recognize it as long as you continue to search for answers. Instead, I suggest you start searching for questions."

"How so?" Mark questioned.

"By focusing on the answer itself," Father Kevin replied.

"And that answer is...?" Mark asked, thoughtfully.

"That you've changed. Period. Don't ask why or what you're supposed to do next. You've already done it. You've changed," Father Kevin pointed out. "So stop searching for what you're supposed to do, and just start being."

"But isn't that the question? Who am I now that I've changed?" Mark wondered.

"Not at all. Like I've already said, we believe that questions always come first. But, in life, it's the *answers* that come first. This is why so many people struggle to find meaning. They aren't using the right order of operations."

"What *is* the right order, then?"

"Start with those books you have by your side. Trust me, by the time you're done reading them, you'll have quite a few additional questions to sift through. Somewhere in the litany of all those new questions, you'll find the ones that match perfectly with your answer."

Father Kevin paused, giving Mark some time to reflect. Mark's mind raced. His eyes turned towards the floor as he followed random patterns in the texture of the hardwood. Thinking of the experience as the answer didn't make any sense. He just couldn't grasp the concept. Mark turned his eyes back towards Father Kevin with a pleading expression on his face and shook his head. Still Father Kevin said nothing. Mark took a deep breath and then let it out with an audible sigh.

"I'll read these books like you suggested, Father," Mark began, "but I honestly don't know how much they'll help. There must be something more you can do to help me understand this."

Father Kevin nodded slowly as he took in a deep breath. As he exhaled, his eyes narrowed and his ears pulled back.

"Maybe if I shared some news I learned earlier this week." he said, pausing a moment as if second-guessing himself. "But, please don't repeat this to anyone. It's not yet public." Father Kevin paused again. "Brian is stepping down as Youth Minister at the end of this year. He has received an offer to work with the Office of Youth Ministry at the Diocese. He was going to turn it down, but I insisted he take it. The opportunity he was presented with doesn't come up very often, and he is definitely more than qualified for the role."

Mark pondered the news. At first, he could see no obvious connection to his situation. Father Kevin leaned forward slightly and opened his hands, as if waiting for Mark to respond.

Still perplexed, Mark shifted positions, and then, dropping his voice to nearly a whisper, asked, "Are you thinking of asking me to take his job? To be the new Youth Minister?"

"Funny you should ask," Father Kevin said as he leaned back and folded his hands neatly on his lap, "because your name was one of the first ones Brian offered as a possible replacement."

"Wow," Mark said, rubbing his hands together as he carefully considered how to respond. "I have to admit, I'm a bit flattered. But, to be honest, I don't know if I could even begin to understand what I would do in that role. Are you sure I am qualified? I mean, there's so much about my faith I don't know yet. I'm not sure I'm ready for that."

"Honestly, Mark, I agree. I'm not convinced that the Youth Minister position is the right one for you, either. Instead, I have something else in mind that I think would be a better fit, and would still allow you to stay involved with the youth."

"And what might that be?" Mark asked, his curiosity rising.

"Would you consider becoming a deacon?"

Mark sat back in his chair, "A deacon?"

Father Kevin leaned forward once more, keeping his eyes locked on Mark's.

"It's one of the Holy Orders," Father Kevin explained, "similar to being a priest, except that deacons can be married."

Mark tilted his head slightly, his imagination showing images of himself wearing vestments and celebrating Mass.

"So, I could do the things that you do?"

"Not all of them," Father Kevin explained. "You could perform baptisms and weddings, as long as you are designated to do so. But you wouldn't celebrate liturgy, hear confessions or perform an anointing of the sick, for example. Though you could assist during Mass, like Brother Daniel does from time to time."

Mark placed his right hand on his chin.

"I've never thought about doing anything like this before. I don't know why, I guess it just never crossed my mind," he said. "But, why should I consider it? What benefit would there be for me to pursue this?"

Father Kevin shifted his weight once again, taking a more relaxed position.

"Becoming a deacon would allow you to be a part of the ministry team here and would give you the training and understanding you would need to run a youth ministry program, or any ministry you might choose. It would also allow us to hire someone to manage the daily operation of the youth program under your guidance and supervision." Father Kevin explained.

"Interesting," Mark said, a thoughtful expression on his face. "So, what would I need to do?"

"Well, first of all, you would need to make sure Jennifer supported you in this. She will have to go through the program with you, as if she was going to be a deacon, too. Plus, you would need to take a vow of celibacy. Not in your current marriage, but if something ever happened to Jennifer, you wouldn't be able to marry again."

"That seems like a pretty big decision," Mark admitted, beginning to sense an overwhelming number of questions rising. "And you're sure you've picked the right guy? You really think I can do it?"

Father Kevin sighed, his eyes becoming soft and gentle. It reminded Mark of the look Father Kevin had given him in the hospital. He could tell there was so much mercy inside this man.

"Mark, I honestly believe that what you went through, and what you're going through right now, is leading you into a life of ministry. The relationships you've developed in such a short time, with the teens as well as the adult and young adult volunteers, plus the respect you've earned from the church leadership, is more than credible for someone with less than a year of involvement.

"Think of it this way. If I had approached you last year, before you were in the hospital, and I had asked you to consider becoming a deacon and to help run our youth ministry program, you would have laughed at me, right?"

Mark nodded, a smile creeping across his face.

"Oh, I would have done more than laugh. I probably would have questioned your sanity." he said, chuckling lightly.

Father Kevin laughed.

"See what I mean? But, had you considered it, even for a moment, what question would you have asked yourself?"

Mark pondered for only a moment before his face lit up. With wide-open eyes and a look of understanding on his face, he sat up as straight as he could.

"I would wonder what kind of person I would need to be to accept the challenge. I would wonder what kind of changes I would need to make, what part of me would need to evolve so that I could feel comfortable taking it on," he declared, turning his eyes towards the floor as his thoughts began to churn again.

"And you would most likely start by figuring out what you needed to let go of, what you needed to forgive yourself for, and what you needed to accept about yourself. Isn't that right?" Father Kevin asked, his voice soft and gentle, matching the look in his eyes.

Mark's eyes darted back to Father Kevin. He knew the priest was right.

"That's exactly what I would do," Mark admitted, a bit excitedly.

"And, that's exactly why you are perfect for the Diaconate program. We get people all the time who think they're already perfect. But you're different, which is what makes you more suited for ministry. You don't believe you have all of life's questions answered, nor do you believe you have stopped evolving as an individual. You see the potential in yourself for so much more than you are today, which means you'll be able to help others see the same potential in themselves. And that is one of the things that is sorely missing today with our teens."

Father Kevin paused and shook his head, a wistful look on his face.

"From the feedback I've heard so far from Brian, and even from some of the parents of the teens you've worked with, you're showing them how much value they have. Not at some point in the future when they have everything all figured out, but in the here and now while they're still stumbling over their own two feet in search of who they are. You'll be a tremendous asset to our church, our community, and especially to our teens."

Mark felt his face flush. He had never felt so inspired by an opportunity before. Inspired, and frightened. His mind chewed on that word, frightened. Was he really afraid? This didn't feel anything like the fear he used to feel. Instead of feeling like he wanted to run away, Mark felt like running *towards* the opportunity. He glanced up at Father Kevin, looking for any sign that might help him put his thoughts into words.

"What do you think, Mark?" Father Kevin asked. "Are you interested in learning more?"

Mark took in a deep breath, held it as long as he could, and then let it out. A portion of his anxiousness drifted away with the escaping air.

"I'll admit, I've never been more excited, and yet just as nervous to say yes, than I am right now. I can't find the right words to express what I feel. I'm nervous and excited and anxious at the same time." Mark paused and looked down at the floor, then lifted his eyes back to connect with Father Kevin. "I'm not sure I can give you a response right now."

"Veneration," Father Kevin said, quietly.

"What was that?" Mark asked.

"The word you're looking for is veneration."

"I'm not sure I understand what that means."

"It's a feeling of wonder and awe. Similar to when we say 'the veneration of the saints'. It isn't the same as the devotion we give to the Holy Trinity. It's more of a feeling of reverence and respect."

"Yeah, that's how it feels. I'm not afraid of saying yes and yet I feel like that word alone wouldn't suffice as a response to this opportunity."

"Which is why one of the first things you will do, after you've talked this over with Jennifer, is make a declaration of intent. You're right, a casual response would never be enough. You have to understand that this isn't something you can agree to just to see if it fits. This is a serious commitment.

"Almost every candidate who goes through the program is challenged at one point or another by their own demons. You'll need to be prepared for that. Always remember that it's the ministry, not the minister, which is the most important part. The more you remind yourself of that, the deeper and more powerful your ministry will be."

Mark's shoulders dropped noticeably. After the events of the past few months, what more could he go through? How much stronger would he need to be to face any remaining demons still buried in his past? He would need Jennifer by his side, and he would have to let her carry him, too.

"I'm very much intrigued by this proposal, Father," Mark acknowledged. "And, you're right, I will need to talk this over with Jennifer. One thing I know for sure, she'll like the part about me not being able to marry again."

Both men laughed at Mark's attempt at levity, and then Father Kevin stood up.

"Then, come," he said. "Let's go see when I might be available to meet with you both."

Mark allowed Father Kevin to help him up, and then turned and picked up the books.

"Are you sure it's okay to borrow these?" he asked as they started towards the door.

"I wouldn't have it any other way," Father Kevin told him. "Just do me one favor."

"What's that?" Mark inquired.

Father Kevin stopped walking and grabbed on to Mark's elbow, pulling it slightly towards him to get Mark to turn. He held Mark's curious look for a moment, and then said, "Don't read them."

"Excuse me? I don't understand."

"I mean exactly what I say. Don't read them," Father Kevin continued. "You probably read magazines, you probably read the newspaper. You might even read other books. Reading is informal. It's how you pass the time. That's fine for books that are meant for entertainment or those that help transfer information. But, to truly understand these books, you'll need to do more than that. These books aren't meant to be informative. They are meant to be transformative. They are meant to empower you. Surrender yourself fully to the words contained within. Give up any preconceived notions, give up your judgment and desire to understand, and let yourself be drawn along by what you read.

Mark looked into Father Kevin's eyes, seeing nothing but the seriousness with which he held this promise. He turned his gaze towards the ceiling, considering what to say. After a moment of contemplation, he looked back at Father Kevin.

"Father, you have my word."

At first, Father Kevin didn't respond. He held Mark's gaze, peering deeper and deeper still. Mark felt as though his entire spiritual being was exposed. Father Kevin wasn't judging him on his word alone. He was judging him on the strength of his soul. Finally, just as Mark began feeling nervous once more, Father Kevin smiled. He reached out and held Mark's hand for a moment, patting it gently, then turned and walked out the door, motioning for Mark to follow.

"Good," he said. "Then let's begin."

The story continues in Where Angels Cry

Michael Chrobak has worked with Youth and Youth Ministry programs since he was a teen himself, a long, long time ago. During his career in youth ministry he worked as the Director of Religious Education and Youth Ministry for St. Bonaventure's Parish (Concord, California) and also worked as the Youth Minister for St. Michael's Parish (Livermore, California). He survived raising four children of his own, and continues to stay involved with Youth Ministry through his blogs and books.

How to Connect:

Facebook: facebook.com/michaelchrobakauthor
Twitter: twitter.com/MChrobakAuthor
Instagram: instagram.com/mchrobakauthor
Website: https://michaelchrobakauthor.com